WALKING DEATH

No one in the entire AXE network gave it a second thought when he coolly passed through the tight security at the International Conference in Caracas. No one even glanced at the tall, dark figure who walked into the room where the Venezuelan president and the American vice-president were talking. Everyone recognized Nick Carter, AXE's top Killmaster, the best security money and influence could summon.

As the tall man approached the conference room, the headache began. He knew he was Rafael Chávez, Venezuelan revolutionary fighting for his principles and his people. He knew he had penetrated security disguised as Nick Carter, American Intelligence agent. And he knew that within minutes all would be carnage and no one would ever trace him or his weapon.

Everything was going according to plan—but . . .

NICK CARTER

A Killmaster Spy Chiller

AGENT COUNTER-AGENT

AWARD BOOKS
NEW YORK

Dedicated to

The Men of the Secret Services

of the

United States of America

Titles are also available at discounts in quantity lots for industrial or sales-promotional use. For details write to Special Projects Division, Award Books, 235 East 45th Street, New York, N.Y. 10017.

THE NICK CARTER/KILLMASTER SERIES

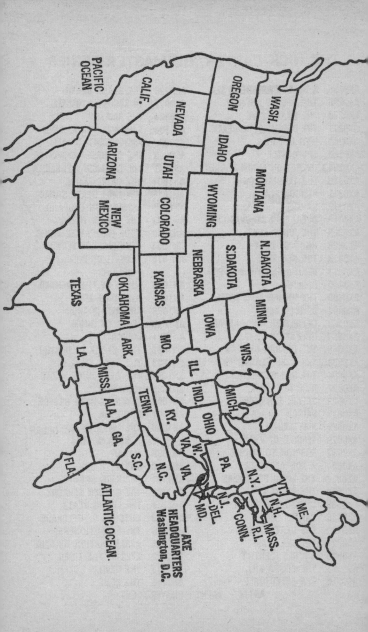

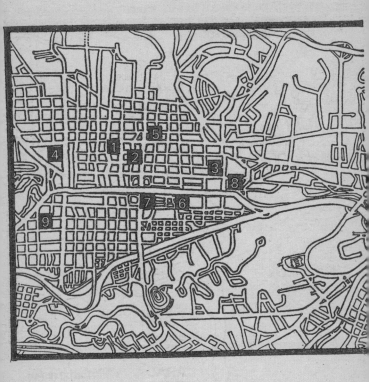

1 Hotel el Conde
2 Cafe
3 Cafe
4 Palacio de Miraflores (White Palace)
5 Cafe at the Plaza Ibarra
6 Nuevo Circo
7 Cafe
8 Restaurante El Jardin

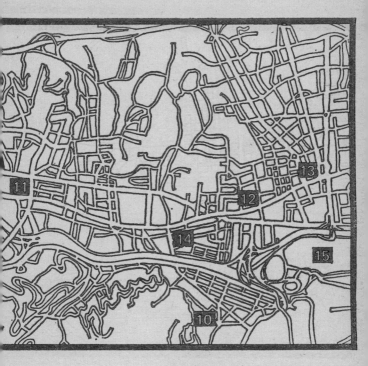

CARACAS/VENEZUELA

One

When pursuing dangerous game, a hunter sometimes finds that he has unwittingly changed roles with his prey and become the hunted. Many wild animals possess the cunning necessary for ambush, like the killer jaguar of Mato Grosso, which hid along its own trail to maul and kill hunting dogs with a swipe of its claws, always killing the last dog in the pack first. And the Dabi rogue elephant, which developed the nasty habit of tearing its human pursuers limb from limb.

Man, of course, is the most cunning of all ambushers, and I considered this fact carefully as I walked along the dark forest path. This was the perfect place for an ambush; and I knew that it had been planned that way.

I walked cautiously, slowly, watching every tree and shrub for movement, listening for any small sound. My Luger, Wilhelmina, lay ready in its holster, but unloaded. The stiletto, Hugo, rested in the chamois sheath strapped to my right forearm, under the jacket I was wearing. I had just moved past an overhanging branch when I heard the sound behind me. Even before I turned, I knew what it meant—a man had dropped from a tree to the ground behind me.

I whirled just in time to see a hand descend with a knife in it. The thin, sharp blade was headed straight for my chest.

Throwing my left forearm up to block it, I grabbed at the man's wrist. At the same time I jabbed the index and middle fingers of my right hand toward the man's eyes. But he jammed his free hand up against the bridge of his nose just in time to save his eyes.

I grabbed his other wrist with both hands, turning and twisting away from him, and pulled hard as I bent forward. The man went flying over my shoulder and hit the ground on his back. The knife flew out of his hand. I tensed a muscle in my right forearm, and my stiletto slid down into my palm. Before the man could move, I stuck the slim point of the stiletto up under his chin and held it there.

"Better luck next time," I said in a low voice.

I didn't drive the knife in under the man's chin as I would ordinarily have done. I held it there while his eyes narrowed on me.

Suddenly he grinned. "Very good, N3," he said.

"Any suggestions?" I asked, moving the stiletto away from his throat.

He sat up and dusted himself off. "Well, I could mention that you should get more of your hip into the throw. And that your stiletto is not regulation issue and is considered inferior to the German Trapper's Companion you just took away from me. But I think you know all that, anyway. And you seem to get the job done, regardless."

I put Hugo back in its sheath. "Thanks," I said.

I had passed the first test of the refresher course. My assailant was the assistant aikido instructor at the AXE training academy, and I had to admit he'd done a damn good job of making sure I remembered the fundamentals of self-defense. We were on the grounds of the AXE supersecret school for agents.

"Now proceed along this path till you reach the intersection with the trail leading back to the training center," he told me. "Expect anything."

"I always do," I answered, smiling.

I left him there and started down the winding path. The moon slid out from behind the clouds, streaking the trail with an eerie silvery light. I moved cautiously, ready for anything. When I got to the intersection, I paused for a minute. I was aware of the absence of insect sounds, which meant there was a good possibility that somebody else was in the immediate area. I had just started along the path leading to the training center when a man jumped out of the darkness into the path directly in front of me. I drew my Luger and beat the man to his weapon. I aimed the Luger at his chest and pulled the trigger. There was a click on an empty chamber.

"You're dead," I said. "With a 9 mm slug through your heart."

The dark-suited figure laughed, and I saw that he was wearing a stocking over his face. The laugh and that stocking set wheels turning inside my head. While I was still trying to figure it out, I heard a slight noise behind me. The man had been only a decoy. But it didn't make sense. The instructors never worked in teams against you, not on the night exercises.

Before I could turn to face the second man, I felt a sudden, sharp pain explode at the base of my skull. Bright lights flashed at me in the blackness. My knees buckled, and the ground came up and smashed into the back of my head. I heard a low groaning somewhere, a rasping sound, and it was coming from my own throat.

"Is that him?" I heard a voice say.

"Yeah, that's him," the other man answered in an accent of some kind.

I opened my eyes painfully and saw the two dark figures swimming in the darkness. They both wore stocking masks. "What . . . is this?" I managed to ask.

"Real life, Mr. Carter," the one with the accent said. "Not games at school, as you thought."

I squinted through pain-blurred eyes to see the shapes of the faces behind the stockings, but it was too dark to see much of anything. Anyway, it didn't require any brilliant deduction to figure out that these were not instructors from the training academy. I was just trying to guess how they'd gotten onto the grounds when one of them kicked me hard in the side.

I grunted and swore under my breath. The pain was excruciating. The man with the accent was aiming a Colt Cobra .38 Special at my face.

"That was just to convince you that this is not a game, Mr. Carter," the one with the Colt told me. The other man was breathing shallowly, and he looked as if he'd love to repeat the lesson.

The kicker put the small automatic back in his pocket. He pulled a black envelope out of his jacket. Making a sound in his throat, he threw the envelope to the ground beside me.

The one with the accent spoke again. "That's a message for your superiors, Mr. Carter. It concerns the forthcoming Caracas Conference. I suggest your people read it carefully and seriously."

My mind whirled in the pain-filled darkness. The conference was a meeting between the American Vice-President and the Venezuelan President that was going to be held at the Palacio de Miraflores, the White Palace, within the next couple of weeks. It was an important political event and was expected to strengthen economic and political ties between the United States and Venezuela.

I wanted to ask questions, to get them to speak some more. But they were through talking. The one who had kicked me before was about to give me one last kick before they left. His trouble was he enjoyed his work too much. This time he aimed his heavy shoe at my head. I grabbed his foot and gave it a vicious twist. I heard the bones crack, and he bellowed as he lost his balance and fell heavily against his comrade. The other man stumbled backward, and they both went down.

"Fool!" the man with the Colt shouted as he scrambled to get back on his feet, trying at the same time to take aim.

By then I was on my feet, and somehow the kicker got himself between me and the gun, which was fine with me. He threw a big fist at my face, but I ducked and it glanced off my jaw. The man with the gun was up on his feet and running into the shadows. I hit the other man, smashing my fist into his temple. He fell onto his back, and I threw myself on top of him, but he got his foot against my gut and shoved. I went flying, and by the time I was back on my feet, he was dragging himself off into the brush.

But I wasn't about to forget how much he'd enjoyed kicking me, and that gave me energy I didn't know I had left. I let the stiletto fall into my hand and threw it after him underhand. It hit him in the back just as he was entering a thick patch of bushes. He yelled, grabbed at his back, and lunged forward onto his face, disappearing from view in the underbrush.

As I walked over to the fallen man, an instructor came out of the shadows behind me. "Hey," he shouted, "what's going on here?"

He came over to where I stood and saw the stiletto sticking up out of the thug's back. "Jesus!" he said. "What the hell happened?"

I pulled the stocking mask off the husky man and saw that he was dead. The face wasn't familiar. "We had visitors," I said. "One got away. He's gone by now."

"You killed this one?" He looked a little sick.

AXE instructors are specialists in self-defense, but most of them haven't spent much time in the field. They train us to kill but are never around for the dirty work.

"It looks as if I did," I said, moving past the slack-jawed karate expert to pick up the envelope my assailants had left with me. I opened it up and could just barely read the message in the dim moonlight.

At the forthcoming Caracas Conference, the government of the United States and particularly the AXE intelligence network will suffer severe humiliation and embarrassment. This is an open challenge to AXE to determine what form the humiliation will take and how it will be executed, and to prevent it if you can. When you fail, the world will see the inefficiency of AXE and the ineffectiveness of the United States government in world affairs.

It was signed simply "The Spoilers." The entire message, including the signature, was pasted up from magazine clippings.

The ashen-faced karate instructor came over to me from the dead man. When he spoke, his voice was cool. "Was that left by these men?"

"That's right," I said.

"May I see it, please?" he asked in his instructor's voice.

"I'm afraid not," I answered.

His face filled with anger. "Now look here, Carter. This unfortunate incident occurred on school grounds. And you have some explaining to do."

I stuck the paper into my jacket pocket. "David Hawk will get a full report."

Everybody at AXE answered to Hawk, even this man's boss at the training center. I suspected that the instructor resented the fact that I reported directly to Hawk. As I started past him to retrieve my stiletto, it looked like he was going to try to stop me.

"Do you think you can take this paper from me?" I asked with a sarcastic grin.

He hesitated for a minute. I knew he wanted very much to accept the challenge, but he was aware of my rank. That single fact frightened him in spite of his black belt in karate.

He moved aside, and I retrieved the stiletto. I cleaned the blade on the dead man's back and returned it to its sheath. "You can take the body to the training center," I said, "but leave it there till you hear from Hawk. And don't remove anything from his pockets."

The instructor just stared hard at me, resentment written all over his face.

"In the meantime, exercises are over," I said. "No more skulking around in the shadows tonight."

I turned away and headed back toward the

buildings. I had to get a call through to Hawk right away.

A couple of days later Hawk and I sat at a long mahogany conference table at AXE headquarters with the head of the CIA, the chief of the National Security Agency, the Secret Service boss, and the director of the Venezuelan Security Police. Hawk had asked these men to meet with us because their agencies were going to provide the security for the Caracas Conference.

Hawk was at the head of the table, speaking through a huge, smelly cigar. "You all have copies of the message before you, gentlemen," he said. "If any of you wish to examine the original again, I have it right here." His spare frame seemed electric with energy, and his hard, icy eyes looked out of place in his jovial Connecticut-farmer's face. I noticed, as I had many times before, that when Hawk spoke, people listened carefully—even these notables.

"There is no lead as to who wrote it?" the CIA chief asked. He was a tall, sandy-haired man with piercing blue eyes and the manner of a five-star general.

"I'll let N3 answer that," Hawk said, shifting the cigar in his mouth.

I folded my hands in front of me on the table. I can't stand these bureaucratic meetings, especially when I have to answer a lot of questions from intelligence brass.

"There's no way to trace the materials that they used for the message itself," I said. "We've checked out the paper, envelope, clippings, and glue, and it's all common stuff that they could have bought at any one of a thousand stores in the area."

"What about the men themselves?" asked the Secret Service head impatiently. He was stocky and blondish, with streaks of gray starting at the temples. He looked very nervous.

"The man I killed turned out to be a shoe salesman in a large department store here in Washington. No leads. He hasn't got a record with any of our departments or with the police. And all I can tell you about his friend is that he's a tall guy with a European accent."

"Russian?" the NSA man asked. He was an older man with white hair and a long, jutting chin. He was doodling on the note pad in front of him, but he watched my face intently.

"I couldn't tell for sure," I said. "It might have been a Balkan accent. And of course it could have been phony."

The Venezuelan drummed his fingers on the table. He was a big man with an olive complexion and dark, heavy eyebrows. He was the man who had successfully protected the Venezuelan government during a series of attempted coups a while back, and he was obviously worried now. "Then we have no idea who is behind the message," he said slowly, in his thick accent.

"I'm afraid that's the present situation," Hawk

admitted. "Even the signature doesn't mean anything to us."

"If it were up to me, I wouldn't worry about it," the NSA chief said. "The whole thing is probably a hoax of some kind."

"Or just some men with a grudge against AXE," the head of the Secret Service commented. "Amateurs who can be handled easily if they show up in Caracas."

"I don't see the Russians or Red Chinese going about an assignment in quite this way," the man from the CIA said slowly. "But then, it's almost impossible to guess how the KGB and the L5 will conduct themselves in any given situation."

"The hard, cold fact remains," Hawk said, "that there is a threat to the conference. The note talks of humiliation and embarrassment, not just disruption. And it is specifically addressed to AXE. What kind of embarrassment would particularly affect my agency, gentlemen?"

There was a short silence. Finally, the CIA chief spoke again. "Your people are often brought in where an assassination attempt is expected," he said, "to block their executioners with yours." He glanced in my direction.

"That's right," Hawk said, sitting back in his chair and glancing around the table. "So if AXE is to be embarrassed at this conference, it's just possible that someone is planning to assassinate our Vice-President or the Venezuelan President or both."

There was a buzz of conversation around the table. The head of the Secret Service regarded Hawk somberly. "I don't see how we can draw that conclusion from the note, David," he said. "I think you're exaggerating its importance."

The NSA man got up from his chair and started pacing back and forth beside the long table, his hands clasped behind him. He looked like a retired British colonel, striding down the room. "I think we're all taking this thing much too seriously," he argued. "The damned note could be a practical joke."

Till now I'd purposely kept quiet. Hawk wanted to hear everyone's opinion before we expressed ours. But now I thought it was time for me to speak up.

"It's a little too well planned for a joke," I said quietly. "Remember, these men managed to gain access to the AXE training-center grounds. And they knew my name and managed to find me there. The one with the accent, who gave me the note, said exactly this: 'I suggest your people read it carefully and seriously.'" I looked around the table. "He didn't sound like he was kidding."

"If I'd killed a man in such a situation, I would want to interpret the whole thing pretty seriously, too," the Secret Service man said acidly.

I couldn't afford to lose my temper. "One of the men held a revolver on me while the other worked me over," I said coolly. "If you'd been there, you certainly would have taken it seriously. I used my knife because I had to stop the man, not because I love killing."

The Secret Service chief just raised his eyebrows and gave me a patronizing smile. "No criticism of your judgment was intended, Mr. Carter. I'm just trying to point out that the intelligence services receive such notes regularly. We just can't afford to take them all seriously."

The Venezuelan cleared his throat. "That is true. But this one seems different to me. And where there is any possibility of an attempt on the life of my President, I cannot take any chances. I intend to double my guards at the Palacio de Miraflores during the conference. And since your Vice-President may also be in danger, I strongly suggest you take extra precautions, too."

"I've just spoken with the Vice-President," the CIA chief spoke up. "He isn't concerned at all. I've told him that all four agencies will have men there, anyway, and he feels that is sufficient."

Hawk looked back at the Secret Service man, who was pressing his clasped hands against his mouth. In spite of his cynical remarks, he was obviously aware that he had the primary responsibility for the life and personal welfare of the Vice-President.

"What do you think?" Hawk asked him.

He regarded Hawk seriously. "Well, I have to admit, it is the lives of the principals to the conference we're talking about here, at least potentially. I'll put extra men on the Caracas trip to match Venezuelan security."

"Good," Hawk said, chewing the cigar. He ran a hand through his gray hair, then took the cigar out of his mouth. "As for AXE, we would not ordinarily have an agent at this kind of meeting. But since AXE was specifically mentioned in the note, I'm sending my top man—Nick Carter—to the conference." He waved a hand toward me. "The Vice-President thinks it would be a good idea if I accompanied him, so I'll go, too."

The CIA chief looked from me to Hawk. "We'll arrange for security clearance for both."

The man from the NSA shook his head slowly. "I still think you're off on a wild goose chase," he said sardonically.

"It may be that," Hawk admitted. "And of course there is a third possibility." He paused, enjoying the suspense. "A trap," he continued, sticking the cold cigar back into his mouth. "The note says that it is particularly AXE that will be humiliated. And that the whole thing is an open challenge to AXE. Maybe somebody wants N3 or me over there for some ulterior motive."

"Then why go?" the NSA man argued. "I would think this is one you'd be happy to sit out."

Hawk chewed the cigar. "Except that that's not the way I operate," he said. "I don't like the idea of hiding my head in the sand and hoping a threat will go away or that someone else will take care of everything for us."

"We welcome your presence, señor Hawk," said the Venezuelan.

The CIA man turned his intelligent, serious eyes on me. "I hope your trip turns out to be uneventful," he said.

I grinned at him. "Believe it or not, I hope so, too."

Two

It was Holy Week in Caracas, and the whole city had turned out for the festival. There were bullfights, parades with colorful floats and everyone dressed in bright regional costumes, concerts and exhibits, and dancing in the public squares. Caracas was letting its hair down for a good time. And yet it wasn't the bright, zany carnival mood that stayed with me as I settled into my room at Hotel El Conde just six days before the conference. It was the cold, spooky feeling of the stiff wind whistling through the narrow cobblestone streets of the old part of the city. I couldn't shake the eerie feeling that the city was trying to tell me something that the festivities concealed from the casual observer. Something evil.

Hawk had taken an earlier flight and was already in the city. He'd thought it was best for us to go separately and stay at different hotels.

I was to contact Hawk at a small restaurant near the American Express office at nine that evening. That gave me a few hours on my own, so I went to a kiosk at the corner and bought a newspaper and a bullfight sheet. I took the papers with me to a nearby sidewalk café, but I decided to sit inside because of the wind. I ordered a Campari and drank it while I read all the stories on the conference, wondering if that forum would be making real headlines before this was all over.

After I'd finished with the paper, I studied the bullfight news. I'd always enjoyed a good *corrida*. When you're in the business of killing and trying to keep from being killed and you live with death —violent death—the bullfight has a special fascination for you. You go, pay your money, and sit in the *barrera*—front row—seats. And you know that there will be a death in the ring, maybe even the death of a man. But whether death strikes the bull or the man, you know that—at least this time —you'll walk out alive. No matter who dies, it isn't you or an enemy you've had to kill. So you sit in your paid seat and take it all in with a sense of detachment you know you'll have to shed as soon as you step back into the world outside the arena. But during the spectacle you can actually enjoy death, smug and aloof from the death that stalks you on the streets.

While I was reading the bullfight paper, I glanced up and noticed a man watching me.

I looked quickly back to the paper. I didn't want the man to know that I'd seen him. I held my eyes on the page and sipped the Campari, watching the man out of the corner of my eye. He was sitting at a table outside, looking at me through the window. I'd never seen his face before, but it occurred to me that his general build was like that of the man with the gun who'd attacked me back at the training center. It might just be the same man.

But there are probably a thousand men in Caracas built like that one. I picked up a movement and glanced up again. The man was dropping some coins on the table, getting ready to leave. As he got up, he looked very quickly at me again.

After the man had gone, I threw some coins onto the table, tucked the paper under my arm, and started out after him. By the time I reached the street, the heavy traffic had blocked him from view. When the traffic cleared, he was nowhere in sight.

Later, at the restaurant near the American Express office, I told Hawk about the incident. As usual, he was chewing on a long cigar. Hawk is a real patriot, but when he has a legal chance to get a hold of a good Cuban cigar, he really can't pass it up.

"Very interesting," he said, thoughtfully, blowing a smoke ring toward me. "It might not mean anything, of course, but I think that we had better proceed with extreme caution."

"Have you been to the White Palace, sir?" I asked.

"I stopped by earlier today. There are a lot of people there, Nick, but there is very little organization. The security people seem more excited about the festival than the conference. I have a bad feeling about it."

"I got the feeling without even going there," I admitted.

"I want you to go to the palace tomorrow and have a long, unobstrusive look around. You have a keen nose for trouble. Use it and report back to me here tomorrow afternoon."

"When does our Vice-President arrive with his party?" I asked.

"Late tomorrow. Our Secret Service boys will be with him. The chief was going to come himself, but he had to go to Hawaii with the President."

"What does the Vice-President have scheduled?"

"There will be several days of sightseeing in and around Caracas with the President and other officials. There will also be banquets and receptions and private talks with the Venezuelan President. Then, at the conference there will be public talks with the Venezuelan President's administrators. The press will be there, of course. The conference will have a morning and an afternoon session. I wish it were shorter."

Hawk ran a hand through his gray hair and stared at the cup of thick coffee he'd ordered earlier. We were sitting at a small booth by the window. The small restaurant was busy, and there was a buzz of Spanish around us.

"When does the Vice-President make his first public appearance here?" I asked.

Hawk flicked an ash off his cigar and looked out onto the dark, narrow street. "Tomorrow night he's scheduled for a gala reception dinner in his honor at the Palacio de Miraflores. After the dinner there will be dancing."

"I'd like to attend that reception, sir," I said.

"I already have invitations for us," Hawk said, chewing on the cigar. "In fact, we have clearance to attend every function that the Vice-President is scheduled for. I don't think we'll need to attend all of them, since the threat was to the conference itself and since the Secret Service boys will be on the job around the clock, tied to the Vice-President's coattails. But we ought to be there at the first function, if just to meet the Secret Service fellows personally."

"We'll go separately?"

"Yes. Everybody but security people will think we're members of the ambassadorial staff here in Caracas. The Vice-President knows our cover and will play along with it."

I could see the worry lines around Hawk's piercing eyes. "You know," I said, "it's just possible that the authors of that warning note aren't planning anything more violent than a demonstration in front of the White Palace."

"Or maybe it really is just a big joke, with somebody sitting back and laughing up his sleeve at us."

I shrugged my shoulders. "Maybe." But I didn't believe it for a moment.

"You're trying to comfort me, Nick. I must be getting older than I thought."

I grinned. "I just want you to relax, sir."

Hawk took the cigar out of his mouth again and snubbed it out in a small ashtray. "I just wish I could get rid of the awful feeling that something deadly is going to happen and take us by complete surprise."

He was staring at the table again. I wanted to say something to break the mood, but I couldn't think of anything. The feeling had gotten to me, too.

Early the next morning I took a taxi to the Palacio de Miraflores. It was an enormous building with about a thousand rooms. The conference was to be held in the Grand Reception Room. The reception dinner and party would take place in the Banquet Room and the Grand Ballroom.

I flashed my credentials at the front entrance and had no difficulty getting in. In fact, it was too easy. The Venezuelan police on duty seemed all too eager to please. The palace had been closed to the public because of the conference, but inside it was crowded with people who had special passes or were in some way connected with the conference.

It was quite a place inside. I was impressed. They'd even left tour guides on duty to help official visitors find their way around. A guide came up to me as I stood looking at a large oil canvas by an unknown Latin American artist.

"*Perdóneme, señor. Siento molestarle.*"

"It's all right," I answered in Spanish. "You're not disturbing me."

"I merely wish to point out there is a Picasso farther down the corridor," the man smiled. He wore a gray uniform and cap and reminded me of a Latin version of Hawk.

"*Gracias*," I said. "I'll be sure to see it before I leave. Have the police set up headquarters in the palace?"

"Yes," he said. "In the state apartments. Follow this corridor and you will come to it."

I thanked him and made my way to the large room that was being used as security headquarters. The atmosphere was hectic, yet casual, if that's possible. Telephones were ringing, and officials were engaged in serious conversations, but other men were joking and laughing and talking about the festival or the *corrida* on Sunday. There seemed to be a good deal of confusion. The Vice-President was expected soon, and the security men were trying to round up a party to go to the airport.

I spoke to a couple of CIA men I knew, but they didn't seem to have much interest in the conference. One of them spent five minutes telling me about a dancer he had met the night before. No one really believed the threat. I left the room and walked through the palace, looking at faces. I don't know what I expected so see—maybe the man who'd been watching me at the restaurant, I don't know. But I was also trying to assess the situation, to get a feeling about the palace and its security, as Hawk had. Unfortunately, my impressions weren't any more favorable than his. I felt like I was sitting on a time bomb that was going to go off when everyone least expected it. It was not a pleasant feeling.

On my way out, one of the CIA agents button-holed me.

"The Venezuelan Security Police have arrested a bunch of radicals, and they'll keep them out of circulation till this is over," he told me. "There's nothing from Washington, no leads on your attackers. Everything looks quiet on all fronts. The scuttlebutt is that the Vice-President isn't taking the note seriously. So why the hell should we?"

I looked at him. "Well, I can think of one reason."

"Yeah?"

"*We're* professionals," I said pointedly. I turned and walked away from him before he could say another word. The new fuzzy-faced bright boys the CIA was hiring nowadays didn't impress me very much.

The Vice-President arrived later without incident. The streets on the route to the hotel where he and his entourage were staying were teeming with welcomers waving American and Venezuelan flags. I was at the hotel to watch the arrival, and it was a noisy one. The head of the Secret Service had kept his promise about extra men. His agents were everywhere. At least *they* seemed to be taking their job seriously.

In the evening I put on a dinner jacket and took a taxi back to the Palacio de Miraflores. It was like Academy Awards night in Hollywood. The streets were jammed with people, and the traffic was impossible. I walked the last long block to the palace. This time there were security people jamming the front entrance. Inside, in the high-ceilinged reception hall, the Vice-President stood surrounded by a few select members of the press.

The Vice-President is a tall man, and he towered over most of the people surrounding him. He was a silver-haired, genteel man, soft-spoken and reserved. His voice was audible only to those closest to him as he answered the reporters' questions. His pretty, dark-haired wife stood beside him in a flowing long blue gown. Again I found myself studying faces, but I didn't see anything suspicious. I was beginning to wonder if the NSA chief hadn't been right. Maybe Hawk and I were taking the whole thing too seriously. Maybe the man at the restaurant was just a Venezuelan who just liked to stare at foreigners. And maybe those men back at the training center had just been trying to scare me with that gun. Maybe.

The banquet was splendid but uneventful. The Venezuelan President appeared in full military costume with a chest full of medals. The Vice-President sat on his right, at the head of the long banquet table. The meal was a superb combination of continental and Venezuelan dishes, and the wine was even better.

A beautiful young girl sat almost directly across from me at the dinner. She was easily the best-looking female at the table, full breasted and slim with long, dark hair and startlingly deep blue eyes. She wore a low-cut black crepe gown that revealed the beginnings of a breathtaking figure. She caught my eye several times during the meal and smiled at me once. Later in the ballroom she came over to me and introduced herself.

"I am Ilse Hoffmann," she said in English, with only a trace of an accent.

She gave me a wide smile, and I couldn't help thinking that the more you saw of her, the better she looked. The clinging black gown emphasized the swell of her full breasts and the spectacular curve of her hips. She couldn't have been wearing anything under the gown, and her erect nipples showed clearly through the clinging cloth. She was taller than I'd imagined, and her legs were long and slim.

"I'm happy to meet you, Ilse," I said. "I'm Scott Matthews."

"I did not mean to stare at you during the dinner, but your face seems so familiar. I work here at the German Embassy. Could I have seen you there?"

"It's possible," I said. "I'm at the American Embassy, recently transferred from Paris."

"Oh, I love Paris!" She smiled again. Her eyes were wide and innocent, and the smile was magnetic for any man with red blood in his veins. She was an incredible-looking girl. "Much more than my native city of Hamburg."

"I've had some good times in Hamburg, too," I said, wondering about her accent. It was basically German, but there seemed to be a trace of something else, too. The music was playing, though, and I didn't waste time thinking about it. "Would you like to dance?" I asked her.

"Very much," she said.

We moved onto the crowded dance floor. A small band was playing at one end of the big room. People were standing and talking in small groups and milling around on the dance floor. I held Ilse very close, and she didn't seem to mind at all. She pressed her warm body against mine and smiled up into my eyes. The effect was sensational.

Halfway through the song, the Vice-President and the Venezuelan President left the ball room for a private talk. A group of plainclothes men went with them. I watched them for a minute, and Ilse noticed.

"I met your Vice-President," she said, "and I like him very much. He is a true diplomat, so unlike the 'ugly American' image."

"I'll bet he liked you, too," I smiled.

"He seems very much a gentleman, a sensitive man," she answered seriously.

The music had stopped. We stood facing each other. I was beginning to wish I'd have more time to myself in Caracas. Ilse could be a very pleasant diversion. "Well," I said, "I enjoyed that."

"You dance very well, Scott," she said. "You have much of the grace of a *torero*. Do you like the bullfights?"

"I see one when I can," I said.

"Ah, another *aficionado!*" she smiled. "I am going to the *corrida* tomorrow afternoon. Carlos Núñez is on the bill, and he is my favorite."

"I like El Cordobés," I said. I knew her remark was an invitation, but I had more important things to do than watch a bullfight. Besides, I had a built-in suspicion of women who took the initiative so quickly in first encounters.

"El Cordobés is my second favorite," she said enthusiastically. Her blue eyes revealed what I'd suspected all along—she was as attracted to me as I was to her. "You ought to go. It will be a fine *corrida.*"

My eyes locked with hers. "Where will you be sitting?"

"In the front row on the shady side," she said. "I'll be alone."

"I'll go if I get a chance," I said. "I'd like to see you there."

"I would like to see you, too, Scott."

I was about to ask her for another dance when I saw the man leaving the ballroom. I only had a quarter-view of his face, but I was pretty sure he was the man who'd been watching me at the café.

"Excuse me, Ilse," I said abruptly and started after the man.

He had already gone through the wide doorway. Some people got in my way and slowed me down. By the time I got into the corridor, I could just see the back of the man's head as he walked briskly toward the front entrance of the palace.

When I got there, he was already outside. I walked quickly past the knot of guests near the entrance, down past the security guards on the steps. I couldn't see the man anywhere. He had disappeared. I went down the steps to ground level and looked past two strolling couples near the end of the building. A dark figure was just turning the corner toward the rear of the palace and the gardens.

I hurried down the walk, then broke into a run when I was out of sight. I stopped briefly at the place where the man had turned the corner. Another walk ran down the side of the building, but there was no one on it.

Swearing under my breath, I ran down the walk, not taking my eyes off the garden area. I'd gone about twenty yards when two men stepped out of the shadows in front of me. One had had a gun in his hand.

"*¡No vaya tan de prisa!*" said the one with the gun. "*Espere un minuto, por favor.*" He was telling me to hold it right there.

They were obviously a couple of the Venezulean Security Police. They didn't know me by sight. The one with the gun was overly arrogant.

"I'm with American intelligence," I said in Spanish. "Did you see a man come along here?"

"American intelligence?" the one with the gun repeated. "Perhaps. Put your hands above your head, please."

"Look, damn it!" I said. "I'm trying to catch the man who came down this walk. He's getting away while you're holding me."

"Nevertheless," the one with the gun said, "I must clear you."

"All right, look, I'll show you my papers," I said angrily.

The other one walked toward me silently, a surly look on his face. I reached for my I.D. just as he arrived. He immediately threw a fist into my face, knocking me down. I looked up at the two of them in disbelief. I had heard that the Venezuelan secret police were pretty tough, but this was ridiculous.

"You were told to keep your hands up!" said the man who had hit me. "We will search you for identification."

The one with the gun held his revolver near my face. "Now you will sit just like that, with your hands supporting you, on the pavement, while we search you."

I'd had enough. I was tired of having to work with an army of blundering security people, and I was especially fed up with the stupidity of these two plainclothes policemen.

I kicked at the gunman's ankle, and the bone cracked audibly. At the same time I grabbed at his gun hand and pulled hard. I didn't care if the damned gun went off and gave everyone a heart attack. But it didn't go off. The policeman went sailing over me and landed hard on his face. I grabbed the gun as he went past and wrenched it from his grasp. The other man dived at me. I rolled away from him, and he hit the pavement. I brought the handle of the gun down onto the back of his neck, and he collapsed in a heap beside me. I got to my knees just as the first man was trying to get to his feet. I stuck his revolver into his face, and he froze.

With my other hand, I pulled my I.D. out of my pocket and stuck it up close to his face so that he could read it. The second policeman was struggling to a sitting position, trying to focus on me.

"Do you read English?" I asked the first one.

He stared at me for a minute, breathing hard, then glanced at his crumpled companion. When he looked back at me, there was a new humility in his face. "Yes," he said. He studied my card briefly. "You are with AXE?"

"That's what I've been trying to tell you," I said impatiently.

He raised his dark eyebrows. "It seems an error has been made."

I got up, and he struggled to his feet. "Now let's see your card," I said quietly. He got it out and handed it to me. While I checked it over, he helped his companion up. The man couldn't put any weight on his right foot. When he realized his ankle was broken, some of the hostility came back into his face. .

The I.D. checked out. They were secret police, all right. I handed the card back, along with the second man's gun. He accepted it silently.

"Okay," I said. "Now we're both satisfied." I started to leave.

"Will you report this?" the man with the gun asked.

I sighed. "Not if you'll quit aiming those things at me," I said, pointing to the revolver. I turned and headed back toward the front of the palace.

The mystery man was gone again. And being a part of this security system was really beginning to get on my nerves.

Three

The next morning I asked Collins, the agent in charge of the CIA operation, to check with the West German Embassy to find out whether they had a girl named Ilse Hoffmann working there. It was Sunday, and the office was closed, but Collins knew the German ambassador personally and was able to call him at his home.

The ambassador said there was a girl named Ilse Hoffmann employed there, and he gave a description that convinced me she was the girl I'd met the night before. The ambassador had sent his deputy to the reception and had told him he could take another member of the staff. Probably Ilse had expressed an interest in going, and the deputy had taken her.

I tried to remember who'd been sitting beside Ilse at the dinner. I seemed to remember that she'd been flanked by middle-aged men. Either of them could have been the deputy. The fact that she was alone later when she approached me was not remarkable in itself. It was natural that she'd want to find more interesting company.

Collins tried to contact the deputy at his home, but there was no answer. The fellow was probably out enjoying himself on his day off.

The girl seemed to check out, but that didn't make me any less suspicious. I still had a bad feeling about this assignment. Hawk had made some recommendations to the CIA and the Venezuelan Security Police. Security now seemed tighter, but the feeling didn't go away. Hawk had it, too. It's not very scientific to have premonitions, but in my business you learn to pay attention to gut feelings. They can develop from a series of small facts that don't amount to enough to jar you on a conscious level but turn on a red light somewhere deep inside you. I don't know. I just know that I've saved my life many times by following my hunches.

Maybe it didn't have anything to do with the girl or even with the man I'd seen at the café and possibly at the palace. It might be something unrelated to them, lurking deep in the shadow of my subconscious. But the girl, and the mystery man were reason enough to be on my guard, premonitions or no premonitions.

I had lunch at a café near the Plaza Ibarra and just off Avenida Baralt. A parade passed while I ate, and I had a good view of it. There were dancers in costume, floats, papier-maché heads on poles, and bands. People were out having fun, and I began to relax a little.

In early afternoon I met Hawk at the restaurant, as instructed. He was sitting outside in the sun, wearing a bright blue sport shirt, open at the neck, with a loosely knotted blue scarf. On his head he wore a navy blue beret, cocked jauntily to one side. He looked like an aging Hemmingway character. I suppressed a smile and sat down across from him at the small table.

"Make yourself comfortable, Nick, and don't make any cracks about the get-up. I'm trying to blend into the holiday crowd."

It was still the same old Hawk under the beret. He pulled out one of his long Cuban cigars, bit a chunk off one end, and spat it out. Then he stuck the cigar in his mouth and turned it slowly, moistening it. The cigar seemed incongruous with the beret and shirt. Finally he lighted it and began sucking it into glowing life. It was a kind of ritual with him, and it never ceased to amaze me.

"You're beautiful, sir," I said, despite his admonition.

He shot a hard look at me. "Not as beautiful as that raven-haired beauty I saw you dancing with last night. What do you think this is—a paid vacation?"

"She insisted," I said. "She seemed quite interested in me."

"Yes, I know," he said. "You've either got it or you haven't." He gave me a wry grin.

"Actually, she put me on my guard," I said, remembering. "I had her checked out this morning but she seems to be okay."

"Anything else interesting at the reception?" he said, working hard at the cigar. "I mean, besides the girl?"

I told him about the man and my encounter with the Venezuelan Security Police. "Of course, I can't be sure it was the same man," I said. "Or if it was, that he has anything to do with the threat. There isn't necessarily anything wrong with a man going to the same café and reception that I went to in the same day. Maybe I'm just jumpy."

A waiter came, and we both ordered Pernod. We didn't resume our conversation till he'd brought the drinks and left again.

"The girl practically asked me to meet her at the bullfight this afternoon," I said when he was gone.

Hawk's eyebrows raised. "Really?"

"She said she's an *aficionada.*"

Hawk began chewing on the cigar, his lean face somber, his bony frame hunched over the table. "What did you tell her?"

"I told her I'd get there if I could. But I have other things on my mind. I want to get back to the palace this afternoon to see what I can find out about my mystery man."

"That's a refreshing attitude," he said, trying not to smile. "I sometimes get the impression that you have a difficult time squeezing work into your busy sex life."

"Just stories circulated by bitter KGB men to discredit me," I smiled.

He grunted. "Actually, when you get on a case you are very tenacious. But I want you to be especially careful on this case. It may be very dangerous for you."

"Any theories?"

He sat there pensively for a minute before he spoke. The warm afternoon sun glistened on his gray hair and touched his face with color. "Nothing special. But if that man who attacked you at the training center was KGB and if he should happen to be the fellow you've seen here twice, it could mean they're setting you up for something."

"With a little luck they could have killed me at the training school."

"Maybe that wouldn't have suited their purpose," he said slowly. He looked up at me. "What time does that bullfight start?"

"At four. It's supposed to be the only event in Venezuela that starts on time."

He glanced at his wristwatch. "You have plenty of time to make it."

"You want me to meet the girl at the bullfight?"

"Yes, I do. I think we'd better find out just what her interest in you amounts to. If it's strictly amorous—well, enjoy yourself, but be discreet. If it's not, we want to know about it."

"All right," I said. "The *corrida* it is."

"Report back to me tomorrow morning. I'll be viewing the Picassos at the Museo de Bellas Artes at ten A.M. tomorrow.

"I'll be there," I said.

If you've never been to the Nuevo Circo at three-thirty P.M. on a Sunday in festival time, you'll never know what complete chaos looks like. There are so many *aficionados* milling around that it's practically impossible to walk from one point to another without having to fight your way through them. There are scalpers everywhere, selling tickets at twice or three times the normal price. Vendors of all kinds clog the open area in front of the arena, and hundreds of pickpockets are hard at work. I had a hard time finding a scalper with a ticket for the shady *barrera* section where Ilse had said she would be sitting. Front-row tickets aren't easy to come by during festival time. But finally I got a ticket and went in.

Inside the atmosphere was completely different. It was still noisy, but there was a kind of hushed expectancy in the crowd, very unlike pre-game time at American football games. I found my seat, which was right down by the ring, where you can see everything at close range. Just then a bugle sounded, and a man on a horse rode across the ring and doffed his hat toward the presidential box. He was the official in charge, and he was obtaining permission from the president of the bullring to proceed with the *corrida*

I looked around for Ilse, and after a few minutes, I spotted her, sitting just two sections over. She hadn't seen me. A man renting cushions came down the aisle beside me, and I bought one. Without a cushion those stone bleachers can be pretty uncomfortable. For a few minutes the two seats beside me were empty, but then an English couple came down and took them. The parade of *toreros* was over, and the band had stopped playing. A silence had fallen over the bullring. I glanced over at Ilse again, and she seemed to be looking around for me.

Then a gate opened, and a big black bull came thundering out of a chute. The bullfighters stood behind the barrier and watched somberly as the bull charged the *burladero* shield just in front of them, smashing into the wood and splintering it loudly. Ilse's favorite, Núñez, was one of the men watching. He was the first *torero* on the bill.

The English lady beside me seemed to be all right through the initial *verónicas* and *rodillazos* with the big red cape, because it was all so colorful and pretty. And she actually seemed to enjoy the graceful *banderilleros*. But she started to get pale when the bull knocked the *picador*'s horse down and almost gored the *picador*. Núñez fought the bull, and his capework was good, if a little flashy. Finally he went in for the kill, and the blood flowed. On the first try the sword hit bone, and he had to pull it out. But the second attempt was more successful—the blade went in clean. Núñez' *cuadrilla* chased the bull in circles till it fell to its knees, and the *matador* finished it off with a dagger at the base of the skull. Then a team of mules came out and dragged the crimson-splattered carcass past us on the way out of the ring.

By then the English lady had had enough. She was really green as her husband led her away.

Núñez was taking his bows around the ring. He had been awarded an ear more out of respect for his reputation than for his performance. He hadn't deserved it for that fight. His capework had been pretty good, but he hadn't killed the bull well. Instead of going in over the horns, which is necessary for a good kill but requires a certain amount of courage on the part of the bullfighter, Núñez had stabbed at the animal like an apprentice butcher.

After the shouting died down a little, I called to Ilse. She turned at the sound of my voice, and I waved to her.

"There are empty seats here if you'd like to join me," I yelled.

She didn't wait for a second invitation but immediately started to make her way over to me. Ilse was wearing a short suede skirt and matching vest over a sheer white blouse. As she moved, the skirt revealed her long, tanned thighs.

"I am afraid my favorite *torero* had a bad day," she said as she sat down beside me. I gave her my cushion.

"Doesn't everybody occasionally?" I smiled wryly.

She returned the smile and dazzled me. "Maybe he will do better on his second bull."

"I'm sure of it," I said. "I'm sorry to have left so fast last night. But I saw a man I knew, and he was leaving."

I watched her face for a reaction, but there was none. I was sure she had seen the man, too, and I wondered if she knew him. But if she did, she wasn't showing it.

"I know that business comes before socializing," she said. "Unless the socializing is business."

I smiled. "Well said."

You can tell when a woman wants to go to bed with you, even if she's trying to hide it from you. Mostly it's the way she looks at you and the gestures she makes with her hands and body. Sometimes she comes on strongest when her conversation is anything but seductive. She can be telling you to get lost or explaining the latest theory in thermodynamics. But her body, her chemistry, always gives her away. Ilse kept talking about the fine points of bullfighting, but I could tell that she wanted me as much as I wanted her. Even if she had ulterior motives for wanting to see me, I found myself looking forward to the evening.

The second bullfighter was just coming out to work his bull, a big, fine bull from one of the best ranches. The *torero* was an unknown, but he was taking chances to please the crowd.

"Olé! Olé!" they yelled.

"He's good," Ilse said.

"Yes." I watched him execute a *mariposa*, making the cape flutter like a butterfly. "Do you know any of the *toreros?*"

"Not personally," she said. "Even though I like to watch them perform, they are not my kind of men, you know. Anyway, Latin men usually do not appeal to me."

"How long have you been at the embassy," I asked, changing the subject.

"Since my arrival in Caracas, almost a year ago. I thought I wanted to see the world."

"And now you don't?"

She turned those blue eyes on me and then looked back to the ring. "It can be . . . lonely for a girl in a strange city this size."

If that wasn't a green light, I'd never seen one. "You went to the reception last night with a bachelor," I said.

"Ah, Ludwig." She laughed. "He is a nice man, but he likes to collect butterflies and read long books on ancient history. I am not even sure he is interested in girls."

We exchanged smiles. "Do you work for him?" I asked. I knew that Ilse Hoffmann did not.

She did not look at me but kept on watching the *torero*. "No, not for Ludwig. For a man called Steiner."

The answer was right, but I still wasn't satisfied. "I know Hamburg quite well. Where did you live there?"

"In the north of the city. On Friedrichstrasse. There is a park nearby."

"Oh, yes. I know the area. Did you live there with your parents?"

"My parents were killed in an automobile accident when I was very young," she said.

That was true, too. The ambassador had mentioned to Collins that Ilse Hoffmann was an orphan.

"I'm sorry."

We watched the bullfight. I bought two drinks from a vendor, and Ilse seemed to be enjoying herself very much. Núñez appeared again and performed better than on his first try. There were just two bulls to go, and the word was that they were immature calves from a second-rate ranch.

"Why don't we leave now and have a drink together somewhere?" she offered.

I looked into her blue eyes and saw the invitation there again. "Sounds great," I said.

We had a drink at a nearby café, and then I took Ilse to dinner at El Jardín, on Avenida Almeda. After we had finished our dinner, she asked me back to her apartment for a drink. Because I still hadn't figured her out and because the seductive promise in her eyes had really gotten to me, I went.

She had a large apartment just off the Plaza Miranda. It was furnished in period Spanish, with some excellent antiques. There was a small balcony overlooking a narrow street.

When we got inside, Ilse turned to me, and standing very close, said, "Well, here we are, Scott."

Her lips were soft and full and within easy reach. I closed the small distance and kissed her. She responded warmly, as if she had been waiting all day. She pulled away reluctantly.

"Make us a drink while I change," she said.

She disappeared into the bedroom. I poured us a couple of cognacs from a crystal decanter, and by the time I'd finished, Ilse had returned. She was wearing a long, clinging robe that didn't leave anything to the imagination. She dimmed the lights, then came over to me and took a cognac.

I had taken off my jacket while she was in the bedroom and hadn't bothered to hide the Luger and stiletto. I watched the look on her face when she saw them. I'd hoped it would be surprise, and it was. But I couldn't be sure it was genuine.

"What is all this, Scott?" she said.

"Oh, just weapons," I said in an offhand manner. "We have to take extra precautions at the embassy when there's something like this conference going on."

"Yes. Of course," she said.

I took in every detail of her body through the clinging material of her robe. I put my drink down. I hadn't even tasted it, but somehow that didn't seem important at the moment. Ilse took a sip of hers and put it down, too. I slipped my hands around her small waist and pulled her to me. Somehow the robe heightened the effect. No small curve or sweep of flesh was hidden from my touch. I kissed her again and she pressed urgently against me as my hands moved over her body.

"Oh, Scott," she said.

I reached down and slowly unbuttoned the robe, letting it drop to the floor. She stood very still, looking into my eyes. Her body was even more spectacular than I'd imagined. Her breath came shallow, moving her full, round breasts. I removed my holster and stiletto sheath and dropped them on a small table near a wide couch behind us. She helped me undress, then went over to the couch and lay down on it.

"Come over here, Scott," she whispered.

I went to her. We lay together on the sofa, and the exciting aroma of her perfume filled my nostrils. Her warm flesh was in my hands and the sweet taste of her was on my lips. She moved insistently against me as my hands and lips covered the swell of her breasts, caressing the erect nipples. Her hand was on me, and it was guiding me to her, and then there was a hot sweetness engulfing me. Her hips undulated against me, and her legs locked around my back. She made low, sensual noises in her throat as our passion mounted. Then she gave a harsh cry, and her soft flesh trembled violently as I exploded inside her.

A little while later, Ilsa got up to get our cognacs. I lay relaxed and satiated on the couch, sprawled out full length. If this was what Ilse had to offer in return for my doubts, it seemed pointless to go on worrying about her.

Still, I watched her carefully and at the same time kept my eye on my weapons on the nearby table. I let Ilse take a drink of her cognac before I took one.

"Did you enjoy it?" she asked me after I had taken a sip.

"The drink or the entertainment?" I asked. Just then I began to feel a little dizzy.

"The entertainment," she smiled back.

"It was first class." As I sat up on the edge of the couch beside her, I felt my arms getting heavy.

"I enjoyed it, too."

I was really beginning to get tense. I was feeling dizzier and weaker, and there was no reason for it. Unless Ilse had drugged me.

"What the hell . . ." I said. The words just wouldn't come.

Ilse didn't say anything. She moved slightly away from me.

I looked over at her. I was suddenly very angry —with her and with myself. I had let my guard down, in spite of Hawk's warnings and my own doubts.

"You bitch!" I said loudly, the words echoing strangely in my ears. I slapped her hard across the face, and she fell back on the sofa with a muffled gasp.

I got up and reeled drunkenly. I grabbed my clothes and began pulling them on. "What's your real name?" I asked, trying to zip my pants.

She looked at my weapons but didn't have the courage to try for one of them. She wiped a trickle of blood from her mouth. "My real name is Tanya Savitch," she said.

I had my shoes on now. I took a step toward the table where the Luger and stiletto lay and almost fell on my face. I grabbed for the table, but I knocked it over and it crashed to the floor I steadied myself on the arm of the sofa, standing over the girl named Tanya Savitch.

"And you work for the KGB," I said.

"Yes. I am sincerely sorry, Mr. Carter," she said quietly. "I like you."

I glared at her and saw two Tanyas. "It was the cognac, wasn't it? But you drank it yourself. And I watched you when you went to get the glasses. What did you do, stuff yourself with an antidote earlier?"

"It was not the cognac," she said almost unhappily. "It was the lipstick. And I have a hypnotic immunity to its toxic effects."

"Hypnotic . . . ?" I couldn't finish the question. I felt the swelling darkness overpower me, and then I hit the floor.

I didn't care about the weapons any more. I just wanted to fight the blackness and get out of the apartment. If I could even make it to the corridor, somebody might help me. I somehow found enough strength to get back on my feet and stumble toward the door.

Just as I reached it, it opened, and two men stood there. One a short, bald thug, had a stupid grin on his face. The other was the man I had seen at the café and the palace, probably the one who'd held the gun on me back at the training school in Washington. Their faces blurred as the drug really began working. The taller of the two, the one who had plagued me since Washington, stepped toward me.

"You appear to be a little under the weather, Mr. Carter."

I took a clumsy swing at him. He ducked away easily, and I fell against his stocky companion, who grabbed me and held me up for a moment, then hit me hard in the side of the head.

I went falling back into the apartment, landing on the floor again. As the short, stocky man stood over me, I grabbed at his legs and pulled them out from under him. He hit the floor beside me. I could just barely hear the Russian obscenities. The tall man came over and kicked me in the side.

"Don't hurt him," I heard the girl say. "There is no need to hurt him." The voice seemed to come from the other end of a long tunnel or maybe from the other side of the world.

The tall man swore loudly at the girl. The stocky man stumbled to his feet. The vertigo was getting worse and worse. I tried to get to my knees but fell back heavily onto my side. The thing that kept running through my mind was that they had come to kill me. This had been a plot to assassinate AXE's top agent, and it had succeeded. But neither of the men had guns out.

"You think that what we're going to do to him won't hurt him?" The stocky Russian gave an ugly laugh. He kicked me hard in the ribs. I groaned and fell onto my back. I heard the girl named Ilse Hoffmann and Tanya Savitch deliver some well-chosen words to the stocky man. Then the voices faded away and became a dull buzzing in my ears.

A minute later the blackness returned, and there was no pushing it away this time. I was suddenly falling, falling through a bottomless black space, my body turning slowly as I fell.

Four

When I came to, I was lying on the floor of a bright, antiseptic-looking room, about ten feet square. The room was empty except for a white cot. The ceiling lights shot rockets of pain into my head when I looked at them. I struggled to sit up and immediately felt the pain in my side where the men had kicked me. I examined my ribs. There were some nasty bruises, but nothing was broken.

I had no idea how they'd gotten me here. At first I couldn't even remember the events leading up to my blackout, but then slowly the scene with the girl came back. Damned clever of them to put a drug in her lipstick. But what was it she'd said about her immunity? And why did I remember, now, her soothing voice speaking to me in the overwhelming blackness, her sensual, irresistible, voice telling me to sleep undisturbed? The fact was, I'd gone out completely, so completely that I'd have felt refreshed now if it hadn't been for the throbbing pain in my side.

With some difficulty I got up, and went over to the cot, and sat down on the edge of it, rubbing my face with my hands, trying to clear my head. Whatever drug they'd used on me, its effect was temporary and apparently harmless. For some reason I couldn't figure out, they wanted me alive and unharmed. Maybe before it was all over I'd be wishing they'd put a slug in my brain back at the girl's apartment.

I remembered Tanya's warm flesh under me on her sofa. The KGB was big on sex as a weapon, always had been. But that wouldn't have been enough to get me without the new cosmetic drug. There'd been rumors that the Russians were working on hundreds of drugs and that they were many years ahead of the West in that area. I may have been the first enemy agent they'd used the drug on. It wasn't a distinction I wanted to claim.

Looking back on it, I didn't figure Tanya for an ordinary KGB agent. There had been that attempt to keep the men from beating me and that mention of . . . some kind of hypnosis. *Hypnotic immunity*, that was it. I'd never heard the term before. My mind raced through all sorts of possibilities and probabilities and ended up nowhere, and my head throbbed violently. I had just succeeded in thoroughly confusing myself when I heard a sound at the door.

I tensed automatically. The door opened, and the two men who had appeared at Tanya's apartment came in. The fat, bald guy had the same ugly grin on his face. The tall one looked at me impassively.

"Well," the tall one said, "I hope you had a good rest." It was definitely the voice of the man who'd attacked me in Washington.

"It was you with the stocking over your face in Washington." I said.

"Yes, it was I," he said patronizingly. "The man you killed was merely an American who worked for us. He was expendable."

"And you've been keeping an eye on me in Caracas."

"Of course. We did not want to lose contact before Dr. Savitch had a chance to ensnare you."

"*Dr.* Savitch?"

"You'll see her presently," he said. "On your feet now, Mr. Carter. You have an appointment to keep in our laboratory."

"Laboratory?" I stood up and gauged the distance and position of each man, wondering if I could get past them to the door. "Where am I?"

The tall man smiled. "You're still in Caracas. We just brought you to a new KGB facility, Carter—one set up especially for you."

"You talk too much!" the stocky man growled.

The tall man didn't even look at him. "It does not matter," he said coolly.

I wondered what that meant. If they intended to kill me, why hadn't they already done it? So far, none of it made any sense to me.

"What are you going to do with me?" I asked.

"You will find out soon enough. Come on. And don't give us any trouble."

I walked past them to the door, and they followed close behind. I looked up and down the white corridor, hoping to find a door that looked like an exit. It was a short hallway with a door at each end and a couple of others in the middle. I figured the end doors had to be exits. They were closed, but something told me they wouldn't be locked. For one thing, the Russians didn't have any keys on them.

This might be my only chance to escape. There was no guarantee that I'd be in any condition to try five minutes from now. We turned and walked toward a door near the far end of the corridor. It was then that I made my attempt.

I stopped suddenly and stepped back into the stocky man, the one who had enjoyed the physical part of my capture. I stepped down hard on his left instep and heard a crunch and a loud cry of pain. I rammed an elbow into his broad face and felt his nose flatten. He thudded against the wall beside him.

The tall man was swearing and going for a gun in his jacket. He got the gun out, and it looked like the same one he'd aimed at my head in Washington. The familiarity didn't give me any feeling of comfort. I grabbed at the gun hand and caught it. With the other hand I stabbed at his eyes. He blocked the blow and quickly raised a knee sharply to my groin. As it connected, I felt a hideous pain and an violent attack of nausea. I grunted and lost my hold on the gun hand. My reactions were slower because of the aftereffects of the drug, and that gave him a substantial advantage.

I swung a hand at his throat, and he partially deflected it. But it caught him a glancing blow on the Adam's apple. He gasped and fell against the wall. I turned and made for the door at the end of the corridor. I had to leap over the slumped form of the stocky man, who was just trying to get back on his feet. I hoped the tall man would take a minute to recover, but my expectations were short-lived. I was only halfway to the door when the revolver exploded.

"Stop, Carter. Or the next bullet will go through your brain."

It was a persuasive threat. I stopped and leaned against the wall, not looking back at him. My chance for escape was gone. In a minute the tall man had reached me and pushed the revolver into my ribs.

"You are a very nasty fellow, Carter," he said breathlessly, holding a hand to his throat.

The other KGB agent limped toward us. "If it were not for them," he said in fast Russian, jerking his thumb toward another part of the building, "I would kill him right here and now. Slowly and painfully."

The stocky man drew his own revolver and raised it to strike my head and face.

"No!" the tall man said. "Think of the mission."

The stocky one hesitated, a wild look in his eyes. Blood was running from his nose over his lips to his chin. The nose was already swelling across his face. I looked at him and wished I'd been able to kill him. It would have taken only a minute longer, and it would have given me great satisfaction.

The stocky man lowered the gun.

"Come on," the tall one said. "They are still expecting us in the laboratory."

They had strapped me to a large wooden chair. I was in the lab. It was a large room that reminded me of an operating room in a large American hospital, except there was no operating table in sight. Perhaps the chair I was bound to served an equivalent purpose. There were several pieces of electronic machinery in the room, with colored lights blinking on control panels. Two technicians were working at the machines, but otherwise I was alone. The agents had left the room after tying me to the chair.

That chair was a machine in itself. It looked like an electric chair, but the wiring was much more complicated. There was even a headpiece with electrodes sticking out of it. At first I thought that it was some kind of torture device, but that didn't seem to make any sense. Even the Russians didn't go to such lengths just to torture a man, not even to get top secrets. There were more primitive ways, which could do the job just as well as any machine. Anyway, agents aren't keepers of deep state secrets, not in Russia or in the West. I was no exception. In fact, AXE agents had less reason than most to carry classified information, since

AXE assignments ran more toward specific physical action against the other side than investigation and collection of data.

While I was still trying to figure it all out, I heard a door open behind me, and three people came into the room. Tanya was one of them. She was wearing a white smock and horn-rimmed glasses. Her hair was pulled back into a bun, and she looked very grim and determined. She met my eyes and looked into them for a long moment before speaking. I think she was trying to tell me she was sorry about all this but that duty came first.

"How are you feeling, Mr. Carter?" she asked impersonally.

"Not bad, considering," I answered.

Two men flanked her. One was familiar to me because I'd just read his file before I left Washington. He was Oleg Dimitrov, the resident operator for the KGB in Caracas and the man in charge of whatever was going on here. He was of average height, with graying hair and a large mole on his right cheek. His eyes were hard and cold.

"So you are the infamous Nick Carter," Dimitrov said.

"I suppose it would be useless to deny it," I answered.

"Yes, useless. I am Oleg Dimitrov, as you probably already know. This lovely girl who helped us capture you is Dr. Tanya Savitch, Russia's most brilliant behaviorist. And this gentleman is her colleague, Dr. Anton Kalinin."

The white-coated, gray-haired man on the other side of Tanya looked at me over his spectacles and nodded. His stare made me feel like an amoeba under a microscope. I looked from him to Tanya.

"Behaviorist?" I asked.

"That's right, Nick. I hope you don't mind if I call you Nick."

I listened to her voice and realized now why it had not sounded quite German. It was a Russian voice trying to imitate German-accented English. It hadn't been perfect, but it had been good enough to keep me guessing.

"You can call me any damned thing you want," I said. "I don't see that it matters much. It would be nice to know what you intend, though. My curiosity has gotten the better of me. Have you three formed a KGB witch coven or something?"

Tanya smiled, but the men remained stony-faced. Dimitrov spoke first, in a tight, high voice. "The classic American hero, eh, Mr. Carter? The brash joke in the face of danger."

I glared at Dimitrov. "It beats the hell out of crying," I answered angrily.

"We will handle this now, Oleg," Dr. Kalinin said to him.

Dimitrov grunted and left us. I heard the door of the lab open and close again as he left. The two technicians at the machines weren't paying any attention to us. Kalinin came and stuck one of those penlights into my eyes. As he worked, he spoke to me in a quiet voice.

"Dr. Savitch specializes in behavior control,"

he said slowly, peering into the backs of my eyes. "She is one of Russia's foremost authorities on narcotic mind control, hypnotherapy, and general behavior-control techniques."

He put the light down, and I looked over at Tanya.

"It's true, Nick," she said. "We've been experimenting with human behavior control for years. I've done a lot of research in the field. Dr. Kalinin has worked closely with our group, recording and analyzing the physical effects of the treatments on our subjects. He is an eminent physician in our country."

"You're planning to conduct behavior experiments on me?" I asked.

"You are going to be the first man to be controlled by our perfected techniques," she answered, her voice revealing her uncertainty. I was sure now that Tanya hadn't known she would be forced to apply her knowledge and skill in such horrifying activities. Her blue eyes hid behind the horn-rimmed glasses.

"You're going to . . . use me somehow?"

Tanya looked quickly into my eyes and then away again.

Kalinin came to her rescue. "We're going to destroy Nick Carter," he said. "For a time, at least. You will no longer exist as Nick Carter."

I just stared at him. Maybe I'd been right—one final bullet in Tanya's apartment might have been better for me in the long run.

"No longer exist?"

"We're going to perform a personality transplant," Kalinin went on. "You will become a completely different person. And that person will be programed by us, Mr. Carter. As a computer would be programed by a technician. Do you begin to understand?"

I looked from him to Tanya. "My God, Tanya," I whispered.

The blue eyes met mine. She had hardened her beautiful face against me and picked up a vial from a nearby table.

"This is nambulin," she said in a businesslike way, "a drug developed only recently by our laboratories. It is what you would call a mind-altering drug. It has properties similar to LSD, but the effects of our drug are narrower and more limited."

"I can hardly wait to hear," I said sarcastically.

She ignored the remark and continued. "When nambulin is administered, the thought processes are interrupted on a basic level, and the personality is altered. The recipient of the drug becomes very submissive, and he experiences a heightened suggestibility."

"Suggestion," I mused. "So that's it."

"Part of it," Tanya said. "While under the influence of the drug, you will be extremely receptive to suggestion by a trained hypnotherapist. And to behavior-control techniques developed in our years of research."

"To what end?" I asked.

Tanya looked away.

"There would be little point in going into details," Kalinin said, taking the vial from Tanya and filling a syringe with the liquid. "You will remember nothing we've said in this conversation, anyway."

Something about the smug look on his face made me very angry. "Goddamn you," I shouted at him.

His eyes flashed up to meet my gaze, and I thought I saw a tiny flicker of fear in them when he looked at me. "No dramatics, please, Mr. Carter. You will only make it more difficult for yourself."

Tanya had left the chair and gone over to speak with one of the technicians. Kalinin was holding the syringe up in front of his face, pushing the plunger to clear the apparatus of air bubbles.

A violent desperation rose in my chest. It was the closest thing to panic I'd ever experienced. I'd never really feared physical pain or death, but this was different. What they were going to do, in effect, was kill me, destroy my identity, and then use my body for their own ungodly purposes. Just thinking about it made chills run up and down my spine. And I knew now that the threat to humiliate AXE hadn't been an empty one. This plan—whatever it was—must have taken them months or even years of preparation. And with a top AXE agent to carry it out, they were almost home free.

A technician came over to assist Kalinin. Tanya turned and looked toward us from across the room. The technician tied a rubber tube around my upper arm and rolled up my shirtsleeve. I saw

the veins standing out in my forearm. The nambulin was going directly into a vein.

My heart pounded wildly. When Kalinin came
toward me with the needle, I started struggling
desperately against the leather straps, trying with
everything I had to break them. If I could get out
of that chair, I could easily take care of these men.
But the bonds were too strong.

"There is no need to struggle, Mr. Carter," Kalinin said smoothly as he grasped my forearm. "Escape at this point is quite impossible."

The needle came down, and the technician held
my shoulders so I couldn't move. There was just a
small hint of pleasure in Kalinin's face as he
jabbed the needle into an enlarged vein, then
pushed the plunger on the syringe.

Five

A feeling of euphoria was coming over me. Then I began to get numb. My breathing slowed down markedly, and I felt perspiration dripping from my forehead and upper lip. I didn't even care that I'd been drugged, and the awful feeling of panic had disappeared. I could still remember everything they'd said to me, and I knew they were going to use me in some horrible experiment in terror, but I was no longer concerned about it. I knew I should be, but I simply didn't care about anything. For a few minutes I fought the feeling, trying to rekindle the rage I'd felt inside me, but there was none left. Whatever they did, whatever they said, was all right with me. It was silly to fight it, to worry about it. I was in their power, and their power was enormous. I would submit to it, and maybe somehow I would survive. After all, that was what really counted in the long run.

Their faces warped in front of me—Tanya's

and Kalinin's—and they were staring at me as they would stare at a guinea pig in a cage, but I didn't mind. They had their job to do, and I'd let them do it.

Kalinin reached toward my face and lifted my eyelids. He nodded to Tanya and then he left us. Tanya brought a straight chair up and faced me. She sat very close. I stared into her brilliant blue eyes and found a dimension I'd missed before.

"Now you are feeling very relaxed, very much at ease," she said to me in a soft, sensual voice. The voice, the inflection, increased my feeling of well-being.

"Yes," I said, gazing into the deep blue pools of her eyes.

"As you look into my eyes, your own eyes are becoming tired. Your eyelids are becoming very heavy, and you want to close them."

My eyelids fluttered.

"It is a struggle to keep your eyes open now. When I count to five, you will close your eyes because you want to. You will feel greatly relieved when you close your eyes. After you close them, you will slowly slip into a deep trance. One. You are very sleepy. Two. Your eyelids are very heavy. Three. You are deeply relaxed and submissive. Four. When your eyes close, you will let my voice guide you in your responses and actions. Five."

My eyes seemed to close of their own volition. I knew that I couldn't keep them from closing, but I didn't even want to try.

"You are now in a hypnotic trance, and you will respond to my voice."

She was speaking in a soft, quiet monotone that was somehow extremely persuasive. I found that I felt tremendous affection for the lovely sound of her voice—that sensual, cajoling voice—and I wanted to do whatever it asked of me.

"Do you understand?" she asked.

"Yes, I understand."

"Good. Now we are going to place this ring device onto your head and attach the electrodes." I felt someone moving the piece of equipment onto my head. It fit like a headband, and I remembered the maze of wires that had run from it.

"As I speak to you, Nick, you will receive audio-visual data from the machine. The things you see and hear will be pleasant and will assist you in reaching the deepest state of trance." I heard a button click somewhere, and then a swirl of beautiful colors assailed the blackness Tanya had created. Along with the colors came a soft swell of music, beautiful music I'd never heard before. And Tanya's voice accompanied the lovely sights and sounds.

"All the muscles of your body are gently relaxing, easily relaxing, and a great sense of euphoria is engulfing you. You are on an escalator that is moving downward. With each foot you move slowly downward, and you are becoming even more relaxed."

The machine created the escalator for me, and

in a smooth-riding glide I was carried down through the maze of colors toward a soft darkness.

"You are nearing the bottom of the escalator now, and you are going in a very, very deep trance. You are completely receptive to my voice." I reached the bottom, and I was in a magnificent, free-floating blackness I never wanted to leave.

"I will now ask you to count to five, but you will skip the numeral *three*. You will not be able to speak the number *three*. Now count to five."

My lips moved. "One, two, four, five." My mouth and brain would have nothing to do with the number *three*.

"Very good," Tanya said. "Now tell me your name and who you are."

Something deep inside me balked, but there was that all-powerful voice asking me, so I answered, "I am Nick Carter. I am employed by AXE, where I have the code name N . . ." I couldn't remember the number, and a rating of Killmaster." I went on to give more details of identification.

"All right. Now listen to me carefully. You are going to forget everything you have just told me and everything else connected with your past. You are at this very moment developing complete and total amnesia."

A strange thing happened. An exotic tremor passed through me, and when it was gone, I felt very lightheaded. When the physical effects passed, I felt different. It was a subtle difference, but it was as if the whole world around me had disappeared. There was nothing left in the universe except my floating body and Tanya's voice.

"Who are you?"

I thought for a minute. Nothing came. I tried harder, but I still couldn't answer. I had no identity. I was an entity floating in a vast blackness, waiting to be named, classified, and categorized.

"I don't know," I said.

"Where do you live?"

"In this blackness," I responded.

"Where have you come from?"

"I don't know."

"All right. I will refresh your memory. You will now see the image of a man before you." The machine hummed, and I did see a man. He was tall, with dark hair and gray eyes. "The man is you," she continued. "You are Rafael Chávez."

"Rafael Chávez," I said.

"You are a Venezuelan who spent a few years in the United States. You were born in Margarita and educated in Caracas. You have been engaged in several lines of work, but now you are an active revolutionary."

"Yes," I said.

"You live in an apartment at Avenida Bolívar, 36, here in Caracas."

"Avenida Bolívar, 36."

She went on to tell me that I had no family or friends and that the people I associated with were the few in this building, who were comrades in the revolution.

"You will learn more about yourself later," she

finally said. "For the time being, you must rest. I will count backward from five. During the count, you will rise slowly from your trance and float back up into awareness. Five. You are moving back up the escalator. Four. You are completely rested, but you are becoming more aware. Three. When your eyes open on the count of one, you will remember nothing prior to closing your eyes, nothing at all. Two. When your eyes open, you will remember only what I have told you about your identity as Rafael Chávez. You will remember nothing prior to the onset of complete amnesia. One."

I opened my eyes. A girl was sitting there, and I knew I had seen the face before, but I had no idea under what circumstances. It must have been just before I closed my eyes. I noted immediately that she was not Venezuelan, and that lessened my interest in the pretty face. I spoke to her in fluent Spanish.

"*Qué pasó?*" I asked.

"You have been under a light sedation, señor Chávez. You were in an accident and received a blow on the head, and we are taking care of you for a couple of days. You do recognize your revolutionary comrades-in-arms, don't you?"

I looked around the room. A technician unfastened the bonds that held me to the chair and took something off of my head. "Why . . . yes," I said. The fact was, I remembered almost nothing.

"This is Dr. Kalinin, and I am Tanya Savitch, your Russian friends in the revolutionary movement. These other fellows are Menéndez and Salgado. They have been with you in the movement for some time. We have brought you here to this private clinic to treat you. After all, the conference is not far off."

"The conference?" I asked.

Tanya smiled. "Do not try to remember it all at once. You must go to your room and rest now."

"Yes," I said numbly. "Rest. I feel very tired."

It was pleasantly quiet in the room they took me to. There was just a cot to lie on, but under the circumstances I couldn't expect a hospital bed. After all, I was a man wanted by the law, wasn't I? Frankly, I couldn't remember very much. I wished I had asked the girl how the accident had happened, because I had no memory of it. One thing was clear—I needed these comrades who were nursing me back to health. I needed them very much. They had no idea how bad my amnesia was. Well, it would clear up in a few hours. A good sleep would fix me up fine. But it bothered me that I couldn't remember the important conference the girl had mentioned. My brain whirled with trying to remember, but finally I went to sleep.

I woke up suddenly in the middle of the night. Was I hallucinating, or had it just been a strange dream? It must have been a dream. I was in some foreign country, a desert country. I was running down a dark, cobblestone street, and I was chasing a man. I held a long, black gun in my hand, a German make, probably a Luger. I was shooting at the man and trying to kill him. He turned and fired back at me, and I felt a searing pain in my side. The gun in my hand suddenly turned into a short-handled axe. Then I woke up.

It was an odd dream. I had no memory of being in any country except Venezuela and America. And I had never shot at a man in my life. Or had I? None of it made any sense to me.

When morning came, they brought me a tray of food, and I ate ravenously. After I'd finished, I examined my face in a mirror. At least it was familiar. But it did not seem to be a face that went with Rafael Chávez. I took a look at the clothing they brought in for me, but I didn't recognize it. The pockets were empty, and there was no identification. About an hour later Menéndez came and took me back to the room with the wired chair and other equipment.

"Good morning, señor Chávez," the girl who called herself Tanya greeted me. "Are you ready for another treatment?"

"Yes, I suppose so," I said, eying the machinery. "But is all this necessary? I'd like to know what kind of treatment I'm getting."

"Please," Tanya said, showing me to the big chair. "You must trust us, señor Chávez. We are your friends."

I sat down in the chair, but I felt uneasy. I wanted to get out of this building, to roam the streets of Caracas, to return to my apartment on Avenida Bolívar. I was sure those familiar sights would bring back my memory and make me well. I promised myself that if this session didn't bring results, I'd go straight home.

"Now, just relax," the man called Kalinin told me. "I am going to give you a mild sedative." He stuck a hypodermic into my forearm.

A name flashed through my mind. *Nambulin.* Where had I heard that before? Before I could think any more about it, I began to feel a deep euphoria coming over me, and I lost interest in the word and everything else.

Someone adjusted a headpiece on me. I didn't mind. A minute later I heard Tanya's voice.

"You want to close your eyes. You will close them on the count of five." She counted, and my eyes closed. There was a sudden burst of color in the blackness, and I heard some odd music that somehow seemed familiar. The voice ceased, but the colors and music kept on, pulling me down and down. I felt as if I were on an escalator. Then another voice came from inside my head. The voice was telling me all about myself. Every small detail, from the date of my birth to my recent activities in the leftist movement to free Venezuela from the tyrannical imperialism of the United States. There were images of specific scenes. When it was over, I had a detailed picture of my past. My amnesia was cured.

I was a member of a political group called the Vigilantes, whose aim was to overthrow the Venezuelan government and to set up a leftist regime with the help of the Russians. I had been recruited several months back and had been injured a couple of days ago in a demonstration at the American Embassy.

Tanya began to speak again. "Your leader has asked us to inform you that the ranks of the Vigilantes are thinning because of cowardly desertion in the face of brutal police tactics. Therefore, action is required now. You have been chosen to carry out the action.

"Venezuela has become much too dependent on the United States," she continued. "The United States buys about 40 percent of Venezuela's petroleum exports, which gives the Americans an economic death grip on Venezuela. The President of Venezuela and his capitalistic government must be destroyed before they turn the entire country over to the Americans. A plan has been devised involving the forthcoming Caracas Conference.

"The conference will be a meeting between the President of Venezuela and the Vice-President of the United States. It will afford a unique opportunity to strike out against both these enemies of the people. You will be advised later as to the nature of the plan and the details of how it is to be accomplished. Do you understand?"

"Yes, I understand."

"Good. When you awake, you will remember in detail all I have told you and all you have heard and seen while in the deep trance. If questions arise in your mind about details, your subconscious will provide the answers and fill in any gaps that may bother you. You will not question your iden-

tity as Rafael Chávez, nor will you doubt the va-
lidity of his political philosophies."

A few minutes later my eyes opened naturally,
and I remembered Tanya counting backward from
five to one. I also remembered everything about
my past life. Whatever they'd done to me, it had
worked. I had completely recovered from my amnesia.

"How do you feel, comrade?" Tanya smiled.

"Quite well," I answered. "The drug made me
remember. I'm to take part in a mission against
the Caracas Conference, I remember it now. Will I
be ready?"

"You will be ready," she said.

Kalinin turned away and went over to a technician at the far end of the room, leaving Tanya and
me alone. "Have you and I . . . do we know each
other better than I remember?" I asked. I had a
fleeting image of Tanya lying nude on a sofa.

There was something in her eyes, then her face
broke into a small smile. "I hoped you would remember. We had an evening together. Don't you
remember it?"

"Not really," I said. "But the glimpse I got
makes me wish I could remember more."

She laughed softly. "Perhaps we will have a few
moments together again before you must leave the
clinic."

"That's something to look forward to," I said.

Even though I felt completely well, they insisted
I stay in my room and rest. I thought about Tanya

for a while. Strange. My mission was the most important thing in my life, yet I couldn't stop thinking about this extraordinary girl.

When I wasn't thinking of Tanya, I was trying to reconstruct the past I had almost lost because of the accident. And as I tried to remember, a small incident came back to me. I was running barefoot into a mud house on the outskirts of Margarita. Then I remembered the house was my home, and the pretty, black-haired woman named María was my mother. She and my father had both died when I was nine. Not long after that I had come to Caracas, where I'd lived with relatives and studied to become a civil servant.

There was still something strange about it all. I could remember things about my past, but those things seemed unreal, the mental pictures faded and misty. And when I stopped thinking about them consciously, they just disappeared into oblivion and didn't seem a real part of me. Surprisingly, my most vivid memories were of the few years I'd spent in America, working on a loading dock.

I spent the entire day in my room. That night Tanya came to see me. She came in quietly and closed the door behind her. I got up from the edge of the cot, where I'd been reading a newspaper about the Caracas Conference. She was wearing a stethoscope and had a clipboard in her hand.

"May I take your pulse?" she asked.

"Of course."

She held my wrist in her small, soft hand. Our

eyes met, and she looked away quickly. She made a notation on her chart, then stuck the stethoscope on my chest and listened for a minute.

"Do you feel any nausea?"

"No."

"Any sweating during sleep?"

"Not that I remember."

My eyes moved from her full lips over the sensuous curves of her body. Again the tantalizing image flashed through my mind—Tanya lying nude on a sofa. Her next question seemed psychic.

"You said you recalled an . . . intimacy between us, Rafael."

"Yes, I did."

"Would you mind telling me what you remembered?"

I smiled. "No. It was you. On a sofa."

Her lovely blue eyes avoided my look. I took the clipboard and stethoscope from her and dropped them on the floor. Then I pulled her to me gently. I kissed her, and she responded.

"You did sleep with me, didn't you?" I asked quietly.

She tried to pull away, but I held her. "Rafael, you're not a lover," she protested. "You're a revolutionary. You haven't had time for women."

"I must have found time at least once," I reminded her.

Her eyes found mine. "Yes, at least once." She seemed to be remembering. "Just before the demonstration at the American Embassy. I brought a message to your apartment, and you asked me to stay."

"And we kissed, and I held you close like this," I said, running my hands slowly over the entire length of her body.

"Rafael, please . . ." she protested weakly.

I unbuttoned her uniform to the waist and slipped my hand inside, holding her tight against me. I caressed her breasts and felt her nipples harden at my touch.

"Rafael . . ."

We were kissing again. She stopped resisting and returned my kiss with a sudden, tremendous passion, her body straining urgently against me as my mouth explored hers. When the kiss was over, we were both breathless and hungry for more.

"Oh, God, Rafael," she breathed

She slipped out of her uniform and let it drop to the floor. I watched as she pulled her panties down over her long, smooth thighs. She went to the cot and stretched out, her body trembling with excitement. I undressed quickly and lay down beside her. My fingers and lips moved over every inch of her hot, quivering flesh.

Suddenly she tried to pull away, but I held her tight. "What am I doing to you?" she cried. I smothered her words, probing deep into her mouth with my tongue. She began to respond again.

I didn't know what she meant, and I didn't care. All I could think about was her ripe, warm body. She moaned with desire as I rolled over on top of her. Her thighs opened for me, and I could feel her fingernails raking my back. I thrust brutally into her, and she cried out with pleasure. Then everything was darkness and urgency and mounting, uncontainable passion.

Six

I was strapped in the chair again, and the room was completely dark. They had given me another injection but this time there were no cajoling voices. There was only the drug working its way into me. Tanya and Kalinin were not even in the room.

They had mentioned something about the "last phase." I'd heard them say it in Russian, and somehow I'd understood, though I had no memory of ever having learned Russian.

As I sat in the chair, an image appeared in the darkness before me. It was the President, and he was giving a political speech. He was just twenty feet away from me, gesturing as he talked. He was saying things that upset me very much. I broke out in a cold sweat. The euphoria gave way to intense anger as the President's words became more and more abusive, louder and louder. His face slowly warped and became hideously distorted. In a minute the face was all that was left of the image. It began expanding, growing larger and uglier as the venom spewed from his twisted lips. The face was so close I thought I could reach out and attack it.

I heard a scream in the room and realized it had come from my own throat. I had reached out savagely for that awful face, trying to tear into the flesh with my bare hands, clawing at it with my fingers.

But I couldn't reach it. The scream had been one of complete frustration and abject despair at not being able to reach the awful face and destroy it. In another minute the voice died away, and there was just silence as the contorted face continued to move in front of me.

Suddenly Tanya's voice came out of the darkness. "This is your enemy. This is the man who stands between your people and freedom. He is a vile, ugly animal, and he feeds on the carcases of his people. You have always disliked and feared him, but now you are consumed with a desperate, violent loathing. You hate him more than you have ever hated anyone or anything in your life."

I thought my chest was going to explode with the repulsion and hatred I felt for the twisted face. I kept remembering the President's vile words, and I clenched my fists until my nails tore the flesh of my palms.

Finally the image disappeared into the blackness and was replaced by another. This was not familiar to me at first, then I remembered it from the newspaper. It was the American Vice-President. He was speaking in English, but I understood him perfectly. He was explaining that he would work closely with the Venezuelan government, that the United States would offer more economic and military aid to keep the Venezuelan President in power. As he spoke, his face changed. His eyes became more and more evil, and his mouth spewed forth hideous, detestable words.

When the lights finally went on, I was covered with sweat. The technician unstrapped me from the chair and took me back to my room. The drug and the overpowering emotions had completely drained my energy. My legs were so weak that I could hardly walk.

Back in my room, the technician helped me onto the cot and then stared down at me. "Are you all right?" he asked.

"I think so."

"This is all necessary for your mission." He said kindly.

I took a long, deep breath. "Where is Tanya Savitch?"

"She is busy on the project."

"I have to see her."

"I'm afraid that is impossible."

I looked up at him. He was a young Venezuelan, the man called Salgado. His face looked honest. Maybe because of the frankness I saw there, I blurted out a something I hadn't even realized I was thinking.

"Am I really who they say I am? Is all this really necessary for the people's revolution?"

His eyes narrowed on me. "Do you doubt it?" he asked anxiously.

"I . . . I don't know. I guess not. Sometimes I think I am going crazy."

"You are not insane. In fact, you are quite well now." His voice was soothing.

"How long have I been here in the clinic?" I asked.

He hesitated as if wondering whether he should answer me. "You were brought in by a comrade the night before last."

"And when will I be ready to leave?"

"Today."

I propped myself up weakly on my elbow. "Really?"

"The last phase will be over later today. You will have a few more orientation sessions. The next one will not be very pleasant for you, but it will be over before you know it. It is an absolutely necessary part of your preparation for the job at the conference."

"What is that job?"

"They will tell you later today."

Suddenly the door opened, and Dr. Kalinin walked in. He scowled at the technician. "What is it? Why are you still with señor Chávez?"

"He wanted to talk for a moment." The technician sounded frightened.

"Get back to your work," Kalinin said curtly.

"Yes, of course." Salgado turned and left the room.

I watched Kalinin approach me. I didn't like the

idea that the Russians were in charge here and that my own countrymen weren't allowed to speak with me. A Venezuelan should be in control of his own revolution, yet Kalinin had treated Salgado like an inferior.

Kalinin gave me a stiff smile. "I am sorry to take Salgado from you so abruptly, señor Chávez, but he has duties elsewhere. Are you feeling well?"

"Just fine," I answered.

He took my pulse and didn't say anything for a while.

"Very good. You should rest now, and we will come for you after lunch. You have a rigorous session coming up."

"Do I really get to leave this place late today?"

My question took him by surprise. But after a brief pause he answered, "Yes. Tonight you will be ready."

"Good," I said. "I hate confinement."

"So do we all," he said deliberately. "But we must make sacrifices for the good of the revolution. Isn't that so?"

I nodded. Kalinin smiled tightly and left.

I fell asleep for a while. Suddenly I heard my own scream. I sat upright on the cot, soaked with perspiration and shaking all over. I ran a trembling hand over my mouth, staring at the opposite wall. It wasn't like me to be afraid—I knew that much about myself. It must have been the drug they were giving me. I'd had another nightmare. I'd seen the ugly faces from the dark room and heard the harsh, evil voices. It was all mixed up with images of myself. I was stalking through a dark alley with a Luger in my hand. I turned a corner, and suddenly an enormous, warped face loomed up in front of me. It looked like the President's and yet wasn't his—it was a deformed face hanging suspended in the blackness. I fired the Lugar over and over, but the hideous face only laughed at me. The mouth opened, threatening to engulf me. The long, sharp teeth were coming at me. That was when I'd screamed.

After a light lunch I was taken back to the room with the machines—the orientation room, they called it. The technician had warned me that this session would be different, and he hadn't been exaggerating. Tanya met me in the room as the technicians were strapping me into the chair.

"This will be unpleasant," she said. "But it will be over before you know it."

"I thought of you earlier," I said. "I asked for you, but they said you were too busy to see me."

The men finished strapping me in and went over to one of the machines. They hadn't used that one before. It had a small control panel, but there were dozens of blinking colored lights on its counter.

"What they told you was true," Tanya answered.

"Will I see you again after I leave here?"

She looked away. "Perhaps. It all depends on the outcome of the mission."

"I don't know anything about the mission," I reminded her.

"You will shortly."

They used different attachments this time—a wired metal band across my chest and a new headpiece. Tanya saw to it that everything fit properly and then left the room.

They turned the lights out, and I saw more pictures in the blackness. The images were even more real than the ones I'd seen that morning. They hadn't given me an injection this time, but I knew that the effects of the morning dosage still hadn't completely worn off.

The President appeared in the room. He was walking through a crowd, waving and smiling evilly. As soon as the image appeared, the headband began doing something to me. An awful pressure started building up in my head, and the pain became almost unbearable. As I watched the images move, the agony increased. I struggled to get free, opening and closing my mouth and squinting my eyes hard against the pain. It just kept getting worse till I thought my head was going to explode. A scream welled up in my throat. A man separated himself from the crowd and ran toward the President, swinging a huge machete. The blade connected, decapitating the President, and his head went flying into the crowd, spewing blood everywhere. People laughed and jeered.

The pain disappeared, and I felt only the sweet emptiness of physical comfort. The President was dead, and the world was saved from his tyranny.

I hoped the session was over, but it wasn't. Another scene filled the room, with the President making a public speech. The pain came again, and I braced myself against it, coiled inside to steel myself against it. But it overwhelmed me. This time the awful pressure in my head was accompanied by stabbing chest pains, as if I were having a heart attack. I heard myself scream, but the pain didn't go away. A man pointed a pistol at the President and blew the back of his head off. The pain subsided immediately.

But again the room filled with images, this time of the American Vice-President. He was riding in a black Cadillac in an official parade, and I knew that the Venezuelan President was in the car in front of him. The Vice-President was wearing an expensive pin-striped suit, gesturing to the crowd in an imperialistic manner. The pressure came again, but this time there was no tightening of the chest, just the terrible pain in the head. In a sudden explosion of smoke and debris, the Vice-President's car was demolished by an unseen bomb, and everybody in the automobile was killed. A second violent explosion reverberated in the room, and the Venezuelan President's car disintegrated. The pain was gone for good.

I slumped in the chair as they unstrapped me and disengaged the apparatus. Dr. Kalinin was beside me, but I didn't see Tanya.

"The worst is over," he said to me.

When he was through prodding me with his stethoscope, he helped me out of the chair and walked me down a corridor to an ordinary projection room. The far wall had a screen built onto it, and there was a booth at the back of the room for the projector.

Kalinin slapped a loaded Luger into my hand. I looked at it dully, still numb from the brutal session. It was the gun I'd been shooting in my nightmare.

"The drug has worn off by now," Kalinin was saying to me, "and your reactions to the various stimuli during this part of the preparation will be quite natural. You will keep the gun, and you will do whatever you feel like doing."

I just stared at the big automatic. It was a German gun, I knew, but somehow I associated it with the United States. While I was still trying to figure it out, the room darkened and the film began. These were real pictures, probably taken during the last couple of days at the preconference meetings. The film showed the President walking down the path in front of the Palacio de Miraflores, with the American Vice-President beside him. There were cameramen all around them, and the President was talking casually with his American visitor.

As the figures on the screen appeared to move toward me, an overpowering feeling of hatred rose in my chest, and I became aware of an uneasy feeling in my head, a feeling of great discomfort. The pain increased with the feeling of complete revulsion. I didn't see the screen anymore. The men walking toward me became very real. I raised the gun in my right hand and pointed it at the two figures. I aimed at the President first. I was trembling with hatred and pain, and sweat was pouring down my forehead. I squeezed the trigger. The figures kept walking toward me, undisturbed. I was furious. I fired the gun over and over again, and black holes appeared in a tight pattern on the President's chest. In a minute I was pulling the trigger on an empty chamber. Still the two figures kept coming toward me. I hurled the automatic at them, and then in a fit of rage, lunged toward them. I hit something hard and fell heavily to the floor.

The lights came on, Kalinin helped me to my feet. I was breathless and exhausted. Now that the film was over the pain and anger drained away from me.

"Very good," Kalinin was saying in a sugary voice. "Excellent, as a matter of fact."

"I want . . . out of here," I said to him.

"All right," he said. "We shall not need you until later today, when you will have your final session. You may return to your room."

They took me back to the white room with the cot, and I lay down heavily. It seemed as if several agonizing, sleepless days had passed since I'd gotten up that morning. I fell asleep for a while. But this time there was no nightmare. Instead, I had a very detailed dream of Tanya. She was nude and in my arms. The warm softness of her body was engulfing me, consuming me with desire. Every sense was aroused—I heard her lovely voice and smelled the intoxicating scent of her perfume. And throughout the dream, in the heat of her passion, she kept saying to me, "I am sorry, Nick. I am sorry, Nick."

I couldn't figure out why she was using that foreign name, but I didn't bother to correct her. I didn't care what she called me. Nothing really mattered but the hot, demanding flesh writhing beneath me.

I sat up suddenly. I thought about Tanya and her use of the foreign name. *Nick*. What did it mean? I'd dreamed about a Luger, then Kalinin had shoved one into my fist. I wondered, as I lay there waiting for them to take me to the final session, whether there wasn't more to these past couple of days than I knew, more than these people were telling me. But they had to be legitimate. They knew all about me, all about my philosophies and my work with the movement. We were all working for the same cause, and I had to trust them.

When they came for me, they told me it was early evening and I would be released within a few hours, after a good meal. They took me to the orientation room but didn't strap me into the big chair. Instead, they asked me to sit in an ordinary chair beside Salgado. After a short time he left and Tanya and Kalinin came in with a third man, a Russian named Oleg Dimitrov.

"Señor Dimitrov works closely with the leader of the movement," Kalinin explained to me.

I looked from the men to Tanya. She was carrying a sheaf of papers under her arm. She smiled uncertainly at me.

"Shall we get started?" she asked impersonally.

"All right," I said. "Let's get started."

They pulled up three chairs and sat down facing me, the men on either side of Tanya. She put the papers on her lap. Dimitrov was staring hard at me, as if trying to assess my innermost thoughts and feelings.

"We are going to ask you to submit to therapy once more," Tanya said. "Then you will be ready."

Kalinin was preparing the syringe. He leaned forward from his chair and gave me the injection. "You will receive only a small amount of the sedative this time," he said, "because we will be releasing you immediately after this session is over." The liquid entered my vein, and he withdrew the needle and pressed a ball of cotton to the tiny wound.

"Now," Tanya said, in her smooth, quiet voice, "you are feeling very relaxed and tranquil." Her voice droned on, caressing my brain, and soon I was in its power. I was completely submissive.

"This time I am going to ask you to open your eyes, but you must not come out of the deep trance. On the count of five you will open your eyes but remain in the hypnotic state."

She counted slowly. When she reached *five*, my eyes came open. I looked from one face to the other. I was perfectly aware of everything around me, but I was still in a state of supreme euphoria.

I was completely relaxed, and I knew I was in the complete power of that voice.

"You have been chosen to carry out the most important mission yet attempted by the revolution," Tanya said gravely. "Day after tomorrow, the Caracas Conference will take place. There will be a morning and an afternoon session. The President of Venezuela, the Vice-President of the United States, and various other dignitaries will be present. The conference will take place at the Palacio de Miraflores.

"You will go to the afternoon session just before the conference is to reconvene. You will be given a water carafe to take into the room. When the conference resumes, a device hidden in the carafe will kill everyone in that room."

A shiver of pleasure passed through me.

"You will not use a gun to kill our enemies, as you tried to do earlier. But you will kill them. Do you understand?"

"Yes. I understand."

"Your face will look different to you when you awake from this trance. We will have made you look like an American spy whose name is Nick Carter."

"Nick Carter," I repeated. *Nick!* That was what Tanya had called me in the dream. It had been a premonition, like the dream about the Luger.

"You will enter the building as Nick Carter. A member of our group will give you a carafe containing a hidden device. You will take the carafe into the conference room and place it on the table.

You will be able to do this because this Nick Carter, whom we have disposed of, has top security clearance at the conference."

"I understand," I said.

"During the next two days you will pose as Nick Carter. I will now begin reading from a file on this agent, and you must remember every single detail so that you will be able to impersonate Carter successfully. Also, you have certain knowledge of this man deep inside you. You may utilize just enough of this knowledge to accomplish your impersonation and no more."

She read from the papers on her lap. The information wasn't difficult to remember. Somehow it seemed very familiar to me.

"It was I who impersonated Ilse Hoffman," Tanya concluded. "After we release you, you will report immediately to Carter's boss, David Hawk. He will wonder why you have been out of touch for two days, and he will ask about me, whom he knows as Ilse Hoffmann. You will say that you took a trip to a country villa with me for a few days because you wanted to check on me but that you are now convinced that I am above suspicion."

"Yes," I said. "Above suspicion." The information was indelibly recorded on my brain.

"You will impersonate Nick Carter as cleverly as you know how, doing whatever is expected of you until noon on the day of the conference. You will then ignore any orders they may give you and go to the palace. You must be in the corridor just outside the conference room at exactly one P.M. At that time our man will approach you. He will be wearing a dark blue suit and red tie, with a white carnation in his lapel. He will hand you this carafe, which is the kind that will be used on the conference table." She took a large, ornate carafe from Dimitrov. "Inside it, under the false bottom, will be this device."

She carefully removed an electronic gadget. It looked like a fancy transistor radio.

"The device is operated by remote control. It emits sound in a wide range of frequencies, wider than anything previously devised. At certain frequencies and levels of volume, sound is destructive to central nervous tissue. Very brief exposure results in painful death."

She replaced the gadget in the carafe. "The device will be tuned to the proper frequency by remote control after the afternoon session has begun. Within minutes it will have killed everyone within hearing range, but it will not affect anyone outside the room. After it has done its job, it will emit a much lower sound, which will still sound very high-pitched to your ears. You will be able to hear that sound outside the conference room, where you will be stationed."

"I will hear the sound outside the conference room," I repeated.

"After our man gives you the water carafe, you will go to the guards at the door of the room and tell them that the palace staff has asked you to deliver the carafe so that there will be fresh water for the members of the conference. Since Nick

Carter has clearance to enter the conference room, they will allow you to take the carafe inside, where you will place it on the table. You will leave it there and take the other carafe to the nearest service room in the corridor. You will stay away from the immediate area until you see that everyone has entered the conference room for the afternoon session. Then you will take up your place just outside.

"When you hear the high-pitched sound from the room, you will know the device has done its job. Now, listen carefully." Dimitrov had gotten up and turned a dial on a small machine on a nearby table. I heard a piercing scream that reminded me of the noise some jets make.

"That is the sound you will hear." Her voice paused a moment. "When you hear it," she said slowly, "you will remember *everything* buried in your subconscious. You will remember everything that I told you earlier not to remember. You will recall all that occurred prior to your coming to this clinic. But you will *not* remember anything that occurred here. This will reveal truth to you but will result in severe confusion. You will admit to the first person who speaks to you that you planted the death device in the conference room. Is this all clear?"

"It is all clear," I said.

"Also, when our man hands you the carafe, he will say, *'Viva la revolución!'* These words will reinforce your determination to kill the Venezuelan President and the American and you will feel an irresistible compulsion to take the carafe into the room as I have instructed you."

"*Viva la revolución*," I said.

Kalinin got up, went over to a table, and got the Luger they'd given me earlier and a stiletto in a sheath. He handed me the weapons.

"Put the gun on," Tanya said. "The stiletto sheath should be attached to your right forearm."

I followed her instructions. The weapons felt uncomfortable and bulky on me. Kalinin brought me a dark suit jacket and a tie, and Tanya told me to put them on over the weapons.

"The weapons belonged to Nick Carter," Tanya said. "You will know how to use them. The clothes were also his."

Dimitrov leaned over and whispered something into Tanya's ear. She nodded.

"You will make no attempt to return to your apartment on Avenida Bolívar. Nor will you contact the Vigilantes or anybody connected with this mission, not even the personnel at this clinic."

"Very well," I said.

"Now, Rafael Chávez, you will come out of hypnosis when I have counted down from five to one. You will speak fluent English, and that is the language you will use until you have accomplished your mission. You will be eager and ready to complete the mission, and you will follow all of my instructions to the letter.

"I will begin the count now. Five. You are Rafael Chávez, and you will change the course of modern Venezuelan history. Four. Your President

and the Vice-President of the United States are
your deadly enemies. Three. You have no thought,
no purpose, but to kill these two men in the manner we have planned. Two. When you awake, you
will not know you have been under hypnosis. You
will not recall the names of those here with you,
but you will know we are friends of the revolution
who have prepared you for your mission."

When she reached number *one*, the threesome
before me seemed to blur for a minute and then
come back into focus. I looked from one face to the
other.

"Do you feel all right, Rafael?" the lovely young
woman asked.

"I feel fine," I answered her in English. Surprisingly, I spoke it with no difficulty.

"Who will you be for the next two days?"

"Nick Carter, the American spy."

"What will you do after you leave here?"

"Report to a man called David Hawk. I will tell
him I was with you—with Ilse Hoffmann—during
Carter's absence."

"Good. Go look at yourself."

I went over to a mirror. When I saw my face, it
looked different. They had altered my appearance,
so that I looked exactly like Nick Carter. I reached
into my jacket and pulled out the Luger. The name
Wilhelmina flashed across the back of my mind. I
had no idea why. It didn't seem important, anyway. I pulled the ejector back and slid a cartridge
into the chamber of the gun. I was surprised at
my facility with the weapon.

I turned back to the three of them. "I don't know your names," I said.

The men were smiling with obvious satisfaction. It was the girl who spoke, though. "You know we are your friends. And friends of the revolution."

I hesitated. "Yes," I said. I aimed the gun at a light across the room and squinted along its barrel. It was a fine instrument. I slipped it back into its holster.

"You appear ready," the girl said.

I held her gaze for a moment. I knew there had been something between us, but couldn't remember her name. "Yes, I'm ready." I felt a sudden urge to get out of there, to get on with the most important thing in my life—the mission these people had prepared me for.

The man in the business suit spoke now. His voice seemed quite authoritarian. "Then go, Rafael. Go to the Caracas Conference and kill your enemies."

"Consider it done," I said.

Seven

"Where in the hell have you been?"

David Hawk was stomping around the hotel room in a black fury. His gray hair was rumpled, and there were deep lines around his cold blue eyes. I didn't know Americans were capable of such fits of rage.

"I was with the girl," I said.

"The girl! For two days? There have been important developments during your untimely vacation. It wouldn't have hurt if you'd been here for a briefing."

"She seemed too interested too quickly," I said. "I had to find out whether she was being used against us somehow. She asked me to a country villa for a couple of days, and I couldn't reach you before we left. After we got to the villa, I didn't have any way to contact you."

Hawk narrowed his steely eyes on me, and I was afraid he was seeing right through my disguise. I felt sure he knew I wasn't Nick Carter and he was just playing games with me.

"Is that the whole story?" he asked acidly.

He wasn't buying it. I had to improvise as I went along. "Well, if you must know, I got sick. At first I thought the girl had poisoned me, but it was just a bad case of the *turista's* disease. I wouldn't have been any good to you even if I had been able to make contact."

His eyes were glued to my face as I spoke. Finally they softened slightly. "Good Lord. We're on the brink of the climax of our biggest mission in years, and you decide to get sick. Well, maybe it's my fault. Maybe I've been pushing you too hard."

"I'm sorry, sir," I said. "But I did have to check the girl out. I'm convinced now that she's above suspicion."

"Well, I guess that's something, even if it is something negative."

"Maybe it was a wild goose chase," I said. "Anyway, I'm back on the job now. What are the new developments?"

Hawk pulled out a long Cuban cigar. He bit off the end and rolled it in his mouth but didn't light it. I had a strong sensation of *déja vu*—Hawk in another setting, doing the same thing. All the premonitions and flashes of impossible half-memories were making me nervous.

"The Vice-President has gone crazy on us. He says we're overdoing the security bit. He's pulled off some CIA men and sent the extra Secret Service boys home. Said it looked bad to the press to have an army of security people around, as if we don't trust the Venezuelan police."

"That's too bad," I said. Actually, it was fine. The fewer Americans around to put on my act for, the easier my job would be when I arrived at the conference.

"Well, there are still a lot of people at the palace with guns in their pockets. I brought N7 over myself when I thought you might be at the bottom of a six-foot hole somewhere."

For the first time, I realized that part of the reason Hawk had been so angry was that he'd been really worried about me. Or, rather, about Nick Carter. Somehow the realization moved me, and I found myself wondering just what fate Carter had met at the hands of the Vigilantes.

"N7—that's Clay Vincent?" I asked.

"Yes. He's put up in a third hotel, Las Américas. I've had him checking into your disappearance." he said sarcastically. "Now he can get onto more important matters. Tonight the Vice-President is attending an unscheduled party that's being given in the gardens of the American Embassy. The Venezuelan President will put in an appearance. Since the conference is tomorrow, I want to begin taking special precautions now, particularly regarding any events not on the original schedule." He chewed on the cigar.

The mention of those enemies of the people made me flare up inside. A hot wave of hatred took hold of me, and I had to struggle to hide it.

One wrong move with Hawk could destroy the mission.

"All right, I'll be there," I said.

"Are you really all right now, Nick?" Hawk suddenly asked.

"Sure, why not?"

"I don't know. You just looked different there for a moment. Your face changed. Are you sure you're not still sick?"

I accepted the excuse quickly. "That could be," I said. "I'm not really myself today." I thought that any moment he would see through my disguise and I would have to kill him with the Luger in my pocket. I didn't want to kill him. He seemed like a good person, even if he was one of the enemy. But anybody who got in the way of my mission would have to be eliminated—there was no alternative.

"Well, you're really not yourself," Hawk said slowly. "I was going to send you over to the embassy to check on a couple of aides who will be at the palace tomorrow, but I don't think you're up to it. You'd better get some rest till this evening."

"That isn't necessary, sir," I said. "I'll be happy to go to the embassy and . . ."

"Damn it, N3! You know better than to argue with me. Just get back to your room and stay there till you're needed. I'll call you when it's time to go the embassy."

"Yes, sir," I said meekly, grateful for the opportunity to avoid any more contact with the Americans than was absolutely necessary.

"And don't contact that damned girl," Hawk shouted after me.

The embassy gardens are beautiful any time, but they were particularly splendid that evening. There were lanterns all around the grounds. Flaming braziers and food tables had been set up for guests. At one end of the garden there was a platform where a band played all evening.

Hawk and Vincent were there with me, but we didn't speak to each other. I had met Vincent in a restroom earlier. We had exchanged greetings, and it was pretty awkward for me. I knew I was supposed to know him, but I hadn't been prepared for a meeting with another AXE man. I'd had to bluff my way through our conversation, and I was afraid I hadn't been convincing. Vincent talked briefly about AXE headquarters and about a previous assignment we'd worked on together. I'd let him do the talking and just agreed with everything he said.

The Vice-President appeared quite early in the evening. I tried to avoid him completely. His face and voice aroused such strong emotions in me that I was sure I'd blow my cover if I met him face to face. I went over to the band and just listened to them play. The music was beautiful, and it made me long for the day when my homeland would be free from tyranny. For the first time in hours I began to relax.

But my luck didn't hold out. I heard a voice behind me, and it was the hideous voice of the American Vice-President.

"Mr. Carter."

I turned and looked into his face and began to feel the horrible pressure in my head, but I fought the revulsion. The Vice-President was flanked by two Secret Service men, who nodded to me.

"Mr. Vice-President," I said tightly.

"You have not met the President, I believe," the monster was saying. He gestured toward an approaching figure, and I saw the man I hated most in the world. He was erect and distinguished-looking, a seemingly harmless old man with a wide smile and a chest full of ribbons and medals. But I knew what he stood for, and it made my stomach churn. He came up and stood beside us. Two plain-clothes policemen and an aid were just behind.

"Mr. President, this is one of the best young men in our security services," the Vice-President said. "Mr. Carter."

"It pleases me to meet you, Mr. Carter."

The proximity of that face made my rage almost uncontrollable. I fought the overpowering impulse to throw myself onto him and tear him to pieces with my bare hands. Sweat popped out on my forehead, and I felt a severe tightening in my chest, which continued to grow and grow. My head ached so much I thought it was going to explode.

"I . . . I am . . ." I gasped and looked away from the two men. I had to get control of myself, but I didn't know how. I looked back, grim-faced. "It is my pleasure, Mr. President," I said.

They were all staring at me as if I'd lost my mind. The security people were studying me carefully.

"Are you all right, young man?" the President asked.

My eyes struggled to meet his. "Oh, yes," I said quickly. "I'll be all right. I've just had a bout with the *turistas*."

The Vice-President was watching my face closely. "You had better get some rest, Mr. Carter," he said quietly. In another minute they'd moved on to speak with the American ambassador.

In sudden desperation I turned to go after them. My hand went into my jacket. I was going to pull the Luger and blow their heads off. But when I felt the cold metal of the gun against my hand, I came to my senses. This was not the plan, and I had to follow orders. I pulled my hand back out and wiped the sweat off on my jacket. I was trembling all over. I looked around to see if anyone had noticed my actions, and when I turned toward the building, I saw my AXE colleague Clay Vincent staring at me. He'd been watching the whole time.

Fighting my panic, I hurried toward the rear of the embassy building, to the men's room. I felt sick and was afraid I was going to vomit. I was still trembling, and my head felt as if it would split open.

In the restroom I ran cold water over my head and leaned heavily against a washbasin. I put the faces out of my mind, and the pain and nausea began to subside. When I turned to find a towel, Vincent was there.

"What's wrong with you, Nick?" he asked.

I turned from him and dried myself. "It must have been something I ate," I answered. "I guess I'm still a little under the weather."

"You look terrible," he persisted.

"I feel all right now."

"Don't you think you ought to see the embassy doctor."

"Hell no! I'm really okay now."

There was a long silence while I ran a comb roughly through my hair.

"I got something in a drink in that café in Beirut when we worked that one together," he said. "Remember? You helped me out of that. I was just trying to return the favor."

Something deep inside my brain responded when he mentioned the Beirut incident. I had a very brief vision of Clay Vincent falling against an old brick wall and my going to help him back on his feet. In a split second the scene was gone, and I wondered if I had even visualized it.

It shook me up. I'd never met Clay Vincent before in my life. How could I remember being with him in Beirut? I'd never been outside of Venezuela except the time I went to the United States. I didn't know a thing about Lebanon. Or did I? Again I had the feeling that there was something about my past they'd kept from me at the clinic. Something very important. But maybe I was wrong. Maybe the drugs had stimulated my imagination so I could invent scenes to help me with my impersonation of Nick Carter.

"Sorry," I said. "I appreciate your interest, Clay."

He smiled briefly, but then the look of concern came back. "Nick, what the hell were you doing out there after they spoke to you?"

"What do you mean?" I asked defensively.

"Well, for a minute, it looked like you were going for that Luger of yours. What was going on?"

My mind raced through several possible answers. "Oh, that. I guess I'm pretty edgy. I saw a guy reach into his jacket, and for a minute I thought he was going for a gun. I felt like an idiot when he pulled out a handkerchief."

Our eyes met and locked as Vincent assessed my answer. If he challenged me, I'd have to kill him right there, and that would mean big trouble.

"Okay, buddy," he said. His voice had softened. "You'd better get some rest so you'll be better by tomorrow."

I looked at him. He was a stocky, sandy-haired man, probably about thirty-two years old. He had an open, honest face, but I knew he could be tough.

"Thanks, Clay," I said.

"Forget it."

For the rest of the evening I tried to stay out of the mainstream of activity. Hawk appeared at one point when everybody was watching a group of dancers and stood beside me.

"Everything appear normal?" he asked without looking at me.

"Yes, sir," I answered. I wondered if Vincent had spoken to him about me.

"There doesn't seem to be any need for you to stay around much longer, Nick," he said. "I'm sending Vincent back to his hotel, too. But I'll see you bright and early tomorrow at the palace. Even though everything seems fine, I still have that feeling about the warning note. Have you spotted that man who was following you around?"

Another unfamiliar scene flashed through my mind—a man standing in a white room holding a gun on me. No, it was a corridor, not a room. I touched my forehead with my hand while Hawk stared at me.

"No. No, I haven't seen him." How did I even know what man he was talking about? Nothing had been mentioned in the file that my comrades had read to me. Unless I had forgotten.

"Nick, are you sure you're okay?" Hawk asked. "With Vincent here, I could probably do without you at the conference."

"I'm all right!" I said somewhat harshly. I glanced at Hawk, and he was regarding me bleakly, chewing on an unlit cigar. "Sorry. But I feel I'm needed at the conference, and I want to be there."

I had tried to keep the raw panic out of my voice. If Hawk pulled me off the security job, it would be impossible for me to carry out my mission.

"Okay," he finally said. "See you tomorrow, son."

I couldn't look at him. "Right."

Hawk moved on around the garden, and I left. I didn't feel like going right back to my hotel. I needed a drink. I took a taxi to the El Jardín because I felt lonely and somehow I associated that place with the girl at the clinic. When I got inside, I was surprised to see her sitting at a corner table. She was by herself, sipping a glass of wine. She saw me immediately.

Nor will you contact the Vigilantes or anybody connected with this mission, not even the personnel at this clinic.

I turned away from her and went to a table across the room. I felt a terrible urge to go to her, to tell her the problems I'd had, to take her to bed with me. But she herself had forbidden me to make contact. A waiter came, and I ordered a cognac. When he left, I looked up and she was standing beside my table.

"Good evening, Rafael." She sat down beside me. She was even more beautiful than I'd remembered.

Her first name suddenly came to me, out of the depths of my subconscious. "Your name is . . . Tanya." I looked into her eyes. "I'm not supposed to know that, am I?"

"No, but I think I know why you do. It's all right."

"I'm not supposed to be with you, am I?"

"I've been asked to contact you. To see how you

feel and to make sure you have been accepted as Nick Carter."

"I've been accepted," I said. "But the one called Hawk is a little too concerned about my well-being. I was introduced to the President this evening, and it was pretty rough for a minute. But I think I've convinced Hawk that I'm all right."

Tanya's lovely face grew somber. "Hawk is the one man who can abort this entire mission. You must keep him convinced in any way you can that you are Nick Carter and that you are able to carry out your assignment at the conference." Her voice was strained and urgent. "It is imperative that you have access to the conference room at the noon recess."

"I understand, Tanya," I said. I wanted to take her in my arms and kiss her. "Come up to my room," I said. "For just a little while. It's . . . important to me."

"Hawk may be watching you," she said softly.

"No, he isn't. Please come, just for a while."

She hesitated for a minute, then reached over and touched my face gently. I knew she wanted me. "I will be there in half an hour."

"I'll be waiting."

Forty-five minutes later we stood in the semi-darkness of my hotel room, and I took Tanya roughly in my arms. I kissed her and her tongue slid into my mouth. She moved her hips up against me.

"Oh, Rafael," she breathed.

"Take your clothes off," I said.

"Yes."

We undressed in the dark. In a few seconds we were both standing there nude, looking hungrily at each other. Tanya was one of the most beautifully built women I'd ever seen. My eyes devoured the full, round breasts, the small waist, curving hips, and long, smooth thighs. And I was captivated by her smooth, sensual voice. The voice that had spoken to me so softly and persuasively at the clinic. There was an extra magnetism between us because of that special relationship. I hungered for the body that belonged to that lulling, inviting voice, the voice that had such power over me.

We walked to the bed together and I kissed her there, pulling her close to me and feeling her taught breasts against me, moving my hands down over the swelling curves of her hips.

We were both breathing hard. I released her, and she lay down on the bed, her full curves creamy against the whiteness of the sheets. I remembered the passionate moments in my room at the clinic. Suddenly I had another memory, the one from the dream I'd had at the clinic. I saw Tanya stretched out on a sofa instead of the bed, her entire body inviting me to join her. Had it just been a dream? Or had it really happened? I was terribly confused.

I got into the bed and lay close beside her, facing her. I touched her burning lips with mine, then moved my mouth across her throat and shoulder.

"Do you have an apartment in Caracas?" I asked between kisses.

"Why, yes," she answered, startled.

"Do you have a wide sofa in the apartment?"

She looked at me, and I thought I saw fear in her eyes. "Why do you ask?"

"That was where we first made love, wasn't it?" I said. "Before the clinic. It wasn't in my apartment, as you told me. My apartment doesn't have a sofa like that one." They had shown me a couple of pictures of my apartment on Avenido Bolívar.

Tanya seemed upset. "Is it important?" she asked.

"Not really," I said, kissing the hollow of her throat. "It just came to me when I saw you lying here."

Her face relaxed again. "You're right, Rafael. It was my apartment. I was just testing you at the clinic to see if you could remember."

"Because of the mission?"

"Because of my female vanity." She smiled and pressed insistently against me.

I stopped worrying about it and forgot everything but the urgency of my desire and the velvet softness of her flesh.

Eight

Hawk, Vincent, and I went to the White Palace early the next morning. Most of the regular security force had been there all night. By six A.M. it was already a madhouse. Hawk told Vincent and me to check out the conference room and adjacent rooms before nine-thirty, when the conference was scheduled to begin. I was very jumpy. It gave me a weird feeling to be making all these security checks, moving so easily among the people who were there for the sole purpose of stopping me. If I hadn't been so nervous, I'd have enjoyed the irony of it all. The security men nodded and smiled at me, never suspecting I was the one who'd see to it that no one left the conference room alive.

Throughout the morning the faces from the orientation room came back to me over and over again, and every time it happened, I'd break out in a cold sweat. The intensity of my hatred was tearing me apart. I wanted to get on with it, to get the job done, to rid the world of those two evil men.

"Well, here it is an hour before conference time," Hawk said to me, "and we have nothing more to go on than we had when we left Washington. Except that we can look for a tall man that nobody but you has seen."

"That isn't my fault," I said sharply.

Hawk studied my face, and I realized I'd done it again. I avoided his piercing eyes.

"Who the hell said it was?" he snapped back.

"I'm . . . sorry, sir. I guess I'm a little edgy because of the conference."

"That isn't like you at all, Nick," he said seriously. "You always keep your cool. That's why I consider you my best. What is it with you, anyway? You know you can level with me."

I looked at him. He had a strange effect on me, and I couldn't figure out why. I liked the man, and somehow I felt very close to him, though I'd never laid eyes on him before yesterday morning. It was weird. "I'll be all right, sir," I said. "You can count on me."

"Are you sure?"

"Yes, I'm sure."

"All right. If you discover anything, you can find me at the security headquarters."

When he left, I felt like punching my fist into a wall. I might look like Nick Carter, but I wasn't acting like him. And Hawk was noticing. If I wasn't more careful, I'd blow the whole mission.

By conference time, the palace was impossibly hectic. The halls were jammed with people. There were hundreds of reporters from all over the world. Flashbulbs were going off every minute, and there was a great deal of shouting and gesturing. When the principals arrived at the conference room, the crowd around them was so thick you could barely see them.

Seeing them again at close range, I felt such hostility, such open hatred for them that I had to turn away. I couldn't even watch them go into the room. After a few minutes everyone was inside, and the big double doors were shut behind them. The conference had begun.

When I'd gotten to the palace and checked out the conference room I'd made a point of noticing the water carafe on the long mahogany table. It was identical to the one I'd be given later, at the noon recess. It had been sitting there on a tray, along with about a dozen sparkling crystal glasses. By noon, whatever water was left in the carafe would be stale, and it would be natural for the palace staff to bring in fresh water for the afternoon session.

The morning seemed a year long. I paced restlessly up and down the long corridor. The other security people looked at me. The halls were full of them. Two Venezuelan guards, one CIA man, and one Secret Service agent stood guard at the entrance of the conference room. Every one of them knew Nick Carter, and no one had given me a second glance when I'd inspected the room earlier.

At about eleven-thirty, half an hour before the recess, the corridor outside the conference room began to fill again. I was feeling the awful tightness in my chest, and my head was beginning to ache. But this time the pain was almost pleasurable. I knew it would disappear immediately after I'd carried out my mission.

Just before recess a CIA agent came up to me. He obviously knew me, and I was supposed to know him. I concentrated, and his face began to look familiar, though of course it wasn't. It was all conditioning, and I didn't have time to worry about how it worked. Still, these confrontations made me nervous. One slip could destroy the whole mission.

"Where have you been, Carter?" the man asked. "We haven't seen you around here for a couple of days."

"Oh. I've been checking out some leads," I said tightly, trying hard to sound natural.

"Leads?"

"I saw a suspicious-looking man at the reception the other night, but it turned out to be a dead end."

"Oh, yeah, I heard about that. I also heard you were shacking up with some German girl for a while. Any truth in that?" he sneered.

The grin suddenly reminded me of the one on the American Vice-President's face when he had introduced me to the President. "Why don't you get lost, you incompetent bastard!" I snarled.

Suddenly I noticed Hawk and Vincent standing just a few feet away, staring at me. I hadn't seen them walk up.

"You ought to keep this one on a leash," the

CIA man said angrily as he walked quickly past Hawk and Vincent and moved on down the corridor.

Hawk stood there studying me for a minute. When he spoke, his voice was calm and quiet. "Come with us, Nick," he said.

"I'd like to be here when they come out," I said. "There could be trouble."

"Damn it, I said to come with us!"

I rubbed a hand across my mouth. I was in trouble, with just a little over an hour to go till I had to meet the man who'd give me the carafe. But there was no way I could get out of going with Hawk. He wasn't giving me any choice.

"All right," I said quietly.

Hawk led us to an empty private room near the security headquarters. When we were inside, Hawk closed and locked the door, then turned to me. Vincent stood off to one side, looking very embarrassed.

"Now," Hawk said in a hard, low voice. "What the devil is going on here? I've taken about as much as I can from you, Nick. You're acting like a maniac."

I gave Vincent an angry look. "You told him about the incident at the party."

"No, I didn't," Vincent said defensively. "But I should have."

"What incident?" Hawk asked.

"Just a little emotional flare-up," Vincent said.

I licked my dry lips. I was glad he hadn't mentioned my going for the Luger. Hawk was sharp. I was sure he already had doubts about my identity. Maybe he'd spotted some defect in my disguise. Maybe they'd left off some mole or scar or something else that had given me away. No, it had to be my fault. I just wasn't acting like Nick Carter.

"All right, what is it?" Hawk asked impatiently. "Why are you so damned jumpy all the time? You haven't been the same person since you came back from that villa."

The answer was easy. I was a different person. Rafael Chávez. But I couldn't tell him that. He was one of the enemy. Both these AXE men were my enemies.

"I just don't know, sir. Maybe it's because this whole thing is so damned frustrating, with the hordes of people milling around and the noise and confusion. And the worst part is knowing something could happen at any minute and we might not be able to do anything about it. This security work isn't my style."

Both men were silent for a minute. Hawk turned away and walked over to a window. "I'm afraid that's not good enough, Nick." He turned back to me. His lean frame seemed to have shrunk even further into his tweed jacket, and his cold eyes seemed to be looking right through me. "Just what happened during those two days you were gone?"

"Just what I told you," I said.

"I don't like to say it, Nick, but I think you're holding something back from me. That isn't like you, either. We've always been very frank with each other, haven't we?"

The pressure was rising in my head and chest. There was less than an hour to go before I had to be out there in that corridor. And David Hawk wanted to talk and talk.

"Yes, we've always been frank."

"Then let's be frank now," Hawk said. "I think something happened when you disappeared, and I don't understand why you're not telling me about it. I know you must have your reasons for holding back, but it would be a hell of lot better for both of us if you spit it out. Does it concern the Hoffmann girl?"

I shot a look at him. "No, it doesn't have anything to do with the girl. Why the hell should it? I told you she was clear. Do you really believe I'm lying to you? Is my loyalty suddenly in question?" I realized I was shouting, but it was too late.

"Take it easy, Nick," Vincent said quietly.

For a minute Hawk didn't say anything. He was staring at me again, piercing me with those hard, cold eyes. The pressure in my head and chest was rising dangerously, and I felt like a bomb getting ready to go off.

"Nick," Hawk said slowly, "I'm taking you off this case." His face suddenly looked old and tired.

A cold chill passed through me. I turned to meet his eyes. "You can't do that," I said hollowly. "You need me here."

"Please believe me when I say I don't want to. You're number one on my list, and you know it.

Your record speaks for itself. But something is very wrong here. The feeling I had when I arrived in Caracas—the horrible feeling that something had gone haywire—is still with me. In fact, it's gotten a lot stronger in the past couple of days." He looked at Vincent. "You feel it too, don't you, Clay?"

"Yes, sir," Vincent said. "I do."

"You've always placed a lot of value on gut feelings, Nick. You've told me so yourself many times. Well, I do too. And right now I have a very strong feeling that you shouldn't be involved in this assignment any more. For your own good as well as for the good of the conference."

"Sir, if you'll just give me a chance to show you I'm all right," I said. "Just let me stay through the noon recess."

His brow furrowed. "Why the noon recess?"

I couldn't look him in the eye. "That just seems like a particularly dangerous time. Once they're safely back in the conference room, it's not likely that anything will go wrong. I'll leave then if you want me to."

"I want you to leave now," Hawk said coolly. "Vincent, go get one of the Venezuelan guards. I'm sending one back to the hotel with Nick, just to make sure he gets there all right."

"That isn't necessary!" I said angrily.

"Forgive me, Nick, but I think it is," Hawk said. His voice was as hard as his eyes.

Vincent had started for the door, and I suddenly panicked. I couldn't let these men stop me from carrying out my assignment. Something clicked inside, and my head cleared. I knew what I had to do. I had to kill them. A hard, cold determination came over me.

I reached quickly into my jacket and pulled out the Luger. I aimed it at Hawk but spoke to Vincent. "Hold it right there," I said sharply.

They were both staring at me in complete shock.

"Have you gone mad?" Hawk asked incredulously.

Vincent had turned back from the door. "Come around here, where I can see you," I said. As soon as he did, I'd kill them both. But I'd have to be quick about it.

"What is this, Nick?" Vincent asked in a low, strained voice.

"The name is Rafael Chávez." I said. "I'm a Vigilante. It doesn't matter now if you know. Nick Carter is dead, and I'm impersonating him. Within the hour, I'll have completed my mission, and everyone at the conference will be dead. Nothing is going to stop me, so move around in front of me, like I said."

Hawk and Vincent exchanged looks. "I saw the secret tattoo on your right arm when you were washing up this morning," Hawk said slowly. "No, you're not an imposter. For God's sake, Nick, put that thing down and talk to us."

His words infuriated me. I aimed the automatic at his chest. But then I saw Vincent lunging toward me.

I whirled around to meet him, but I was a split

second too late. The next thing I knew, he was on top of me, and we were crashing to the floor.

When we hit, Vincent's meaty fist smashed into my face. It was a hard blow, and it dazed me. Then I felt the Luger being twisted out of my hand. I held on with all my strength, but Vincent had the advantage. The automatic fell to the floor. I was recovering my strength, though. I got a foot up against Vincent and kicked him hard in the groin.

He screamed and fell off me onto his back. I spotted the Luger, then started to go for it.

"Don't do it, Nick. I'll have to shoot." Hawk was standing over us, holding his Beretta on me. I looked up past the long silencer and into his eyes, and I knew he was dead serious. I stood up slowly.

"You think you can stop me with that?" I asked in a menacing voice I didn't recognize as my own.

"I'm quite sure I can," he said calmly. "But don't make me do it."

"I'm going to take that toy away from you and kill you with it," I growled. I took a step toward him.

"I'll shoot, Nick," Hawk said. But I could see a hint of fear in his eyes—he was afraid he couldn't kill me.

I was just about to call his bluff when I saw Vincent staggering back to his feet. As Hawk aimed the gun carefully at my chest, Vincent came at me. I grabbed him and dragged him in front of me to shield myself from Hawk's Beretta. Then I gave Vincent a hard shove, and he fell heavily against Hawk. Both men stumbled backward, and the gun went off, making a soft thumping sound. The slug slammed into the ceiling.

I moved quickly, smashing the side of my right hand against Vincent's neck, and he fell away from Hawk, clearing my path. As Hawk was bringing the gun down to aim again, I grabbed his gun arm and pulled, twisting hard as I dragged him toward me. He went flying over my hip and crashed to the floor, the Beretta clattering up against the wall behind him. He was out cold.

I started for the Luger, but just then Vincent tackled me again. I went down but recovered immediately and threw a left hook into Vincent's broad face. His cheekbone snapped, and he crumpled under the blow. He was hurt, but he wasn't finished. I saw his hand go inside his jacket. In a single motion I slipped the stiletto down into my palm and sent it flying just as Vincent was taking aim. The knife sliced in under his ribs, and he gasped, his eyes going wide, and fell over onto his side.

"Jesus, Nick!" Hawk shouted, staring at Vincent's body in disbelief. Hawk had regained consciousness but was still too weak to move. I grabbed the Luger and aimed it carefully at his head. He'd have to die. There was no other way. I tightened my finger on the trigger, but something stopped me. Hawk was staring up at me, defiant and angry—and hurt.

Hatred and fury welled up in my chest. This man stood in my way. I had to eliminate him. My finger tightened again on the hard metal of the trigger. I looked into that lined face and froze, stunned by an unexpected surge of emotion. I didn't know why, but I liked and respected the man too much to shoot. Yet I had to pull the trigger. I broke out in a cold sweat as the conflicting emotions tugged at my fevered brain. I licked my dry lips and took aim again. My duty was clear. David Hawk had to die.

But I couldn't do it. I just couldn't pull the trigger. Maybe I didn't have to kill him, after all. I could tie him up and keep him out of the way till I'd completed my mission.

Hawk was watching my face. He didn't really seem surprised when I lowered the gun.

"I knew you wouldn't kill me," he said quietly.

"Shut up!" I shouted. I was too frustrated and confused to think clearly.

I bound Hawk's hands and feet with his tie and belt. My mind raced. I'd fought like an AXE agent, not an amateur revolutionary. And I'd bound Hawk like a pro, though I knew I'd never done anything like it before. And there was that strange emotion I'd felt for the old man. It didn't make any more sense than the flashes of unknown memories and the crazy dreams I'd had for the past few days.

Again I had the feeling that something was drastically wrong with all of this—with the people at the clinic, the mission I was on, and myself. But there wasn't time to figure it out.

I dragged Hawk to a closet. I hadn't gagged him

because I knew the rooms were completely sound-proof. He just kept staring at me.

"You're drugged or something," he said.

"Keep quiet and I won't kill you," I said harshly.

"You don't want to kill me. Do you really believe you're a man named Chávez?"

"I *am* Chávez."

"That's not true," he said emphatically. "You're Nick Carter. Goddamn it, you're Nck Carter!"

He was making my head spin. The headache was returning—the headache that would go way only after I'd killed my enemies. I glanced at my watch and saw that I only had about half an hour to go. I stuffed Hawk into the closet and slammed and locked the door. I glanced at Vincent as I walked to the door. He looked dead, and for some crazy reason, I was really sorry about it.

I went out into the corridor and was surprised to find it almost deserted. A Venezuelan policeman was going into a security room at the other end of the hall. He hadn't seen me. Obviously, nobody had heard us. But I didn't want to run into anyone. The security people might wonder where I was coming from, or somebody who'd seen me go down the hall with Hawk and Vincent might start putting two and two together. I decided to leave the palace through a side entrance. I could walk through the garden and come back in through the main entrance. Hopefully, the crowds would have dispersed during the noon recess. And anyone who saw me coming in would just assume I'd gone out for an early lunch. I looked around quickly, walked calmly down the hall, and went out through the side door.

Nine

I put Hawk and Vincent out of my mind. My watch read twelve thirty-five—just twenty-five minutes till I had to meet my contact outside the conference room.

I walked briskly through the garden to the front of the palace. Even during this relatively quiet time, there were people everywhere. Cars jammed the streets approaching the palace grounds. The drives were closed off, but guards were letting top-security cars through.

As I rounded the building, I saw hundreds of people milling around outside on the grounds, waiting for the dignitaries to reappear.

I'd just started down toward the crowd when a man walked up to me from a side path, blocking my route. I looked at him and realized it was the CIA man I'd had the run-in with earlier. I couldn't ignore him. That would have further aroused his suspicions.

"Say, Carter, can I speak to you?"

I turned to him casually, trying to ignore the mounting pressure in my chest. My head was throbbing with pain. "Yes?"

"I just wanted to say that I'm sorry about that remark I made. I don't blame you for getting mad."

"Oh, that's all right," I said. "I overreacted. I'm just a little jumpy. My fault." I started to walk away from him.

"No hard feelings, then?" he asked.

I turned back. "No, no hard feelings. Don't worry about it."

"Good." He stuck out his hand. I took it and gripped it for a minute.

He was smiling broadly, relieved. "You know, I can see how this kind of duty can really get to you. It's the waiting and watching, I think. I don't know how the Secret Service people do it day after day, month after month."

I glanced at my watch. It was twenty to one. I tried not to show my emotion. "Yes, they have a rough job. I sure wouldn't want it. Well, I have to meet a colleague. See you later."

"Sure, okay," he said. "Take it easy, Carter."

I turned and walked on down the long path. The sense of mission was so strong inside me now that I couldn't think of anything else. I wasn't aware of anything around me but my path through the thickening crowd. A cluster of aides blocked the sidewalk as I got to the entrance. I shouldered my way through them, and they looked at me as if I were crazy. But there was no time now for amenities. I made my way around a knot of reporters near the main steps and brushed past them. The crowd was getting thicker.

When I reached the stairs and started up them, I was blocked by the hordes. I pushed and elbowed my way through them. I shoved one man up against another, and he yelled something obscene at me. I banged into a woman, almost knocking her down. But I didn't even bother to look back.

I had to get to the corridor in time.

"Hey, watch it, fellow!" someone shouted after me.

I pushed my way slowly up the steps. "Let me through," I demanded. "Let me through, damn it." At that rate I was never going to get there on time.

I was driven by the urgency of my mission, oblivious to everything but the compulsion to get where I was going. At the top of the stairs the crowd was even denser, and the security people were holding everyone up.

I stumbled and pushed into them. A Venezuelan security man gave me a hard look as I brushed past him. But I had to get into the palace. My contact would be expecting me there at one o'clock sharp. And he couldn't wait. The timing had to be perfect.

"Excuse me," I said, moving into them. "Please let me through!" But nobody moved. Everyone was too busy talking about the conference and world affairs to even notice my presence. I shoved into them, squeezing through the mass of bodies.

"Hey, take it easy!" one man yelled.

I moved past him without answering. I was almost through the congested area just in front of the doors. I looked at my watch and saw I had only seventeen minutes to go. I fought my way through to the door, where several Security Police stood guard.

"Yes?" the Venezuelan in uniform said. Neither he nor the plainclothes man with him recognized me.

"I'm with AXE," I said. "Carter."

"Your identification, please."

I wanted to knock the man down and run past him. The throbbing in my head was almost unbearable. I fumbled in my pocket and came up with Nick Carter's wallet. I opened it and found the I.D. and the special pass for the palace. I showed it to the man on duty.

"Hmm," he said. He looked at the photograph on the cards and then scrutinized my face closely. If Hawk and Vincent hadn't been able to tell I wasn't Nick Carter, this man couldn't possibly see through my disguise.

"Would you hurry, please?" I said impatiently.

If anything, the request seemed to slow him down. He studied the card as if it held some flaw that was just waiting for him to detect it. Obviously I'd offended him with my impatience, and he was going to teach me a lesson.

"Where are you billeted, Mr. Carter?"

I had an almost uncontrollable impulse to ram my fist into his smug face. But I knew that would quickly put an end to the mission.

"Does it matter?" I said, clenching my fists as I tried to control myself.

"*Por favor*," he said sourly.

"Hotel El Conde," I said.

"*Gracias, muchas gracias*," he said sarcastically.

I wanted to speak to him in my native tongue, to tell him he was an idiot, the unwitting tool of a malicious tyrant. But I kept quiet.

"Your cards, Mr. Carter." He handed them back to me. "You may enter the palace."

"Thanks a lot," I said nastily. I took the wallet back and hurried past the guards into the interior.

It was much quieter inside. There were a few people in the entrance hall, but they were scattered, and I didn't have any trouble getting past them. I started toward the Grand Reception Room, which was being used for the conference.

There was another security check when I entered that part of the palace, but one of the guards knew me, so it was quick. I moved down the hall to the conference room. I was almost there.

Just then the chief of the Venezuelan Security Police came out of a doorway just a few yards from the conference room. I felt the revulsion churning in my gut, and the pressure was rising in my head and chest. As head of the brutal secret police, he was almost as detestable as the President himself.

"Ah, Mr. Carter!" he said when he saw me.

"Señor Santiago," I responded, fighting to keep my cool.

"Everything is going well, isn't it? It seems that our precautions were unnecessary, after all."

"It does seem that way, sir," I said tightly. A clock ticked in my head. It must have been about eight minutes to one. I had to get away from him.

"I am certain everything will be all right," he said. "I have a good feeling about it. Have you seen señor Hawk?"

"Not since early this morning," I lied, wondering if my face gave me away.

"Well, I am sure I will find him. And I will see you both later to congratulate you on such a successful day." He smiled and clapped me on the shoulder.

"Very good, sir," I said.

He went back into the office room, which seemed to be some sort of annex to the security headquarters. I breathed a sigh of relief and walked on down the corridor to the conference room. I checked my watch, and it said five to one.

I stood across from the open doors, as I'd been instructed to do. Across the hall there were four guards on duty, the same ones who'd been there that morning. They knew me, so I wouldn't have any difficulty getting past them. Just two more minutes to go. An aide came down the corridor and showed his credentials. The guards let him into the room. There were security people all over the place, moving around in the corridor and standing inside the conference room.

I looked up and down the corridor. I was in a lot of pain. The tension and the pressure in my head were mounting rapidly as the minutes passed. I knew the pain wouldn't go away till I'd destroyed my enemies. Yet I had an awful feeling that somehow this was all wrong. It was a gut feeling, a vague, nagging sensation that seemed to come from a hidden corner of my brain. It didn't make sense—any more than anything else that had happened in the past few days. But whatever the feeling was, it was beginning to tug at my conscience even as the urgency of my mission was overwhelming me. I felt as if there were a terrible struggle going on inside my head, and it just might drive me crazy if it didn't stop soon.

I was beginning to wonder if my contact had been detained. But then I saw him—a dark-haired Venezuelan in a conservative navy-blue suit and red tie, coming down the corridor toward me. He looked like an ordinary member of the palace staff, but he was wearing the white carnation in his lapel and carrying the carafe.

My heart pounded wildly against my ribs. In a minute he was beside me, handing me the carafe. "Señor Carter, the conference director asked me to bring fresh drinking water to the conference room during the noon recess." He spoke very loudly, so that anyone around us could hear him. "Since you have special clearance, would you mind terribly taking it in for me?"

"Oh, all right. I'll take it," I said condescendingly.

"*Gracias*," he said. Then, in a harsh whisper, "*¡Viva la revolución!*"

The man walked quickly back down the corridor. I stood there with the carafe in my hands, overwhelmed by terrible doubts and confusion. I had to take the device into the room. It was too late to think of the other feelings. The most important thing in the world, in my life, was to carry that carafe into the conference room and put it on the table.

I went to the doorway.

"Hello, Carter," the CIA man there said. "What do you have there?"

"It seems the conference director wants fresh water on the conference table," I said casually. "And I'm the errand boy."

The CIA agent looked at the carafe. A Secret Service man grinned at me, then also took a look at the carafe. They seemed satisfied. The Venezuelan policemen nodded for me to go ahead and take the carafe into the room.

I carried the carafe inside. Another Secret Service man eyed me as I took the almost empty carafe from the table and replaced it with the one I'd carried in.

"What's all this about?" he asked.

I grinned at him. "You wouldn't want the conference members to have to drink stale water, would you?"

He looked at the carafe and at me, then grinned back. "Glad to see they're making constructive use of you AXE people."

"Very funny," I said.

I picked up the old carafe and propped it under my arm, then glanced back at the one I'd just placed at the center of the conference table. And I heard the words echoing in my brain:

The device will be tuned to the proper frequency by remote control after the afternoon session has begun. Within minutes it will have killed everyone within hearing range.

I turned and left the room.

Outside, I stopped beside the security guards. "I wonder what I'm supposed to do with this?" I said to them, feigning impatience.

"There's a service closet just down the corridor," one of the Venezuelans said.

"Maybe you could sweep the floor while you're at it, Carter," the CIA man at the door laughed. "There's probably a broom in the service closet." He grinned widely.

"What is this. The CIA Comedy Hour?" I asked sourly, as if their jokes bothered me. I couldn't have cared less what they said or did, just as long as they didn't suspect that the biggest security break in years had just been pulled off right under their noses.

I carried the old carafe down the corridor to the closet. Aides and officials were beginning to drift back into the conference room. I looked at my watch and found that it was already quarter past one. The stars of the show, the Venezuelan President and the American Vice-President, would be arriving in a few minutes. And before long the afternoon session would be getting underway. And nobody inside the conference room would suspect that the remainder of his life could be measured in minutes.

Everything was going according to plan.

Ten

After I'd disposed of the carafe, I drifted back down to the conference room. I was just in time to see the Venezuelan President and the American Vice-President coming down the corridor together, the American's hand resting on the Venezuelan's shoulder. They were flanked by Secret Service agents. As I saw them disappear into the conference room, I was overcome by hatred and revulsion.

Inside, photographers were getting some last-minute shots before the conference resumed. It was rumored that some important economic agreements had been reached during the morning session. Undoubtedly they involved financial aid to the Venezuelan regime in return for permission to install American military bases. Without my intervention, this monstrous tyranny would go on forever.

I had just taken up my position across from the still-opened doors when suddenly the chief of the

Venezuelan Security Police appeared beside me. This time his face was somber.

"Mr. Carter, one of your NSA agents just reported to me that you spent a few minutes in the conference room."

I felt a prickling sensation at the back of my neck. The pressure rose again in my head, making my temples throb horribly.

"Yes, sir," I said. My mind raced ahead. Maybe they'd checked and found that the conference director hadn't ordered the fresh water. Or a cautious agent might have found the device by just inspecting the carafe. They might already have removed the device from the room.

"Did everything appear normal to you?" he asked.

The tightening in my chest relaxed a little. "Yes. Everything seemed all right."

"Fine. Would you mind coming with me for just a moment? I would like you to look at this revised list of people with security clearance. It will not take long."

I felt it would be all right to deviate from my instructions to this extent. The conference room doors weren't even closed yet. Anyway, I didn't see how I could refuse. When the chief of the Venezuelan Security Police asked you to do something, you did it. I followed him into the security annex not far from the conference room. A Venezuelan policeman was there when we entered, but he walked out immediately, leaving me alone with the man I hated almost as much as the men I was about to destroy.

"This is the list." Just a quick perusal will suffice to . . ."

The phone on his desk rang. He went to answer it while I studied the list, trying hard to gain control of my emotions.

His face brightened. "Ah, señor Hawk!"

I felt a steel vise closing on my chest.

The Venezuelan's face changed. "What!"

There was little doubt of it. Hawk had somehow gotten loose and was now calling from another part of the palace, not trusting himself to get here in time. He had figured out that I was going to pull something during the noon recess, which was just ending.

"I can't believe it!" the Venezuelan was saying. I reached for the Luger and moved up behind him. "But señor Carter is here with . . ."

He turned toward me just as I smashed the handle of the Luger down against the side of his head. He fell heavily to the floor and lay there unconscious. The telephone receiver dangled beside the desk. I could hear Hawk's voice from the other end.

"Hello? What happened? Are you there?"

I stepped over the inert body and replaced the receiver in its cradle. I went to the door and looked up and down the corridor. There was no one around. I stepped out into the corridor, closing the door quickly behind me. Hopefully, nobody would go into the security annex for a while.

I walked back to the conference room just as they were closing the doors. In minutes the conference would resume, and the lethal device would be activated. I stood across the corridor, tense and acutely aware of the terrible pressure. It would soon disappear—after the device had done its work. A Secret Service agent emerged from the conference room and nodded to the guards outside. He walked over to me.

"Hello, Carter," he said in a friendly voice.

I nodded.

"Well, they're under way in there. I'll be glad when all this is over."

"Me too," I said.

I wanted him to leave, to let me just stand there and wait it out alone. The signal would come soon, and I would know it was all over. Somebody might stagger out of the room to get help, maybe a security man stationed right at the door. But neither the Venezuelan President nor the American Vice-President would make it—nobody at the table would survive.

"Everything seems quiet," the man said. "A little too quiet for my taste. I have this strange feeling. Do you have it?"

"Not today," I said. "I was really worried when I first got here, though."

"Well, I have it. Right at the back of my neck. But things look all right."

"Yes, I'm sure we'll have an uneventful afternoon," I said.

"Well, I guess I'd better go check with the Security Police. See you later, Carter."

"Right," I said.

He started down the hall toward the security annex. Tiny beads of perspiration popped out on my upper lip. If he found the chief of Venezuelan security lying there unconscious, he'd probably try to stop the conference, and that would ruin everything. I wondered if I should go after him. But I had a strong feeling that I had to stay right where I was. Orders were orders. An NSA man came down the corridor from the opposite direction and stopped to talk with the Secret Service agent. I'd gotten a short reprieve. I let out a shaky breath and looked across to the conference room doors. Inside, the afternoon session was getting under way. Any minute the device would be activated.

Suddenly there was a loud, shrill sound over the building. It was the high-pitched scream of jets flying over the palace to salute the Caracas Conference. The sound pierced my eardrums, and something strange started happening inside me.

A jumble of scenes, words, and mental pictures crashed into my consciousness. I saw myself, with a gun, the Luger. I saw strange cities and an apartment that had to be in America. Everything crowded in on me, churning in my brain and making me feel sick and dizzy.

Something deep inside me seemed to force me to get to a window, so I could hear the sound again. But a strong sense of duty held me back. They'd ordered me to remain outside the conference room.

In spite of those orders, I had to get to a window, and slowly, awkwardly, I walked down the corridor to an alcove where I knew I'd find one. I hesitated once and almost turned back to my post outside the conference room but then went on to the window. I shoved it open just as the jets were heading back for a second sweep over the palace.

At first, as they came toward the palace, I didn't hear anything. But then, when they were almost directly overhead, I heard the loud, high-pitched scream of their engines. It dissipated into a roar as they flashed over the building, gleaming in the sunlight.

This time the sound of the jets really jolted me. It was like a tremendous shock wave passing through my entire body. Suddenly I heard Tanya's beautiful voice:

After it has done its job, the device will emit a much lower sound, which will still sound very high-pitched to your ears.

The sound of the jets was still vibrating inside my head. And I heard another piercing sound in my head, almost like the one the jets had just made.

That is the sound you will hear. When you hear it, you will remember everything buried in your subconscious.

Suddenly truth crashed in on me from every

direction. I looked around me, dazed and horribly confused. What the hell was going on? Why had I been posing as a revolutionary named Chávez. I knew I was Nick Carter, that I worked for AXE and I was here to . . . Suddenly I remembered my fight with Vincent and Hawk, and . . . Christ!

The jets were gone. I leaned weakly against the window ledge. What the hell was this all about? Why had I assumed the identity of a Venezuelan I'd never even heard of before? What had made me fight with Hawk and Vincent, when they were just trying to . . . take me off the assignment. The carafe! I'd taken a carafe into the conference room just a few minutes ago, and I'd known it contained a device that would kill everyone in the room.

It was all coming back fast. I hadn't just been posing—I'd really believed I was a man named Chávez. Everything I'd done during the past two days had been for the purpose of assassinating the President of Venezuela and the Vice-President of the United States—the two men I'd been sent to Caracas to protect! I couldn't remember anything before that, but last night I'd met Ilse Hoffmann again and I'd called her Tanya, a Russian name. And she'd known about my deadly mission.

Yes, that was it! I couldn't remember anything that had happened to me between the time I'd gone to her apartment, several days ago, and the time I'd come back believing I was Rafael Chávez. But something was coming back to me about that evening in her apartment. I remembered a feeling of dizziness and nausea. I'd tried to get away, but two men had stopped me. I must have been drugged. And they'd done something to me to make me act the way I had ever since. That was the humiliation they had spoken of in the message. Somehow they were using me to assassinate the conference dignitaries. And "they" were the KGB. Tanya had admitted it. I remembered explaining my disappearance to Hawk, but that was the story they'd told me to give him. I had no memory at all of those two days I was gone, and that was undoubtedly the way they wanted it. That must have been when they'd conditioned me to assume the identity of Rafael Chávez.

I started running from the alcove, around the corner and into the main corridor. I had to get to the conference room. The device I'd planted there might already be working, and it would kill everybody within earshot.

When I got to the big doors, there were three men guarding them, two Venezuelan policemen and a Secret Service agent. The CIA agent who'd been there earlier had left, probably for a short break. The Secret Service agent and NSA man who'd been talking to each other outside the closed door of the security annex weren't there now, and the door was still closed. The Secret Service man had apparently been diverted before he'd found the chief of the Security Police.

I startled the guards at the conference room door.

"I have to get inside," I said. "There's a weapon

in there, and if I don't get it out fast, it will kill everybody in the room."

I started to push past them, but one of the Venezuelans blocked my way. "I am sorry, señor Carter, but we have strict orders not to interrupt the conference."

"Get out of my way, you idiot!" I shouted.

I shoved the guard aside, but his companion pulled a gun and stopped me. "Please, señor Carter," he said quietly.

"What is it, Carter?" the Secret Service agent asked, looking worried.

I turned to him impatiently. "Remember the water carafe I took in earlier?"

He thought a moment. "Oh, yes." His eyes narrowed. "What the hell's in it, a bomb?"

"No, but something just as bad, maybe worse," I said. "I have to get the damned thing now."

I started in a third time, and the Venezuelan jammed the revolver hard against my back. "Why did you take the carafe into the room in the first place, Mr. Carter?"

It was obvious they were going to make me explain everything before they'd let me in. And there wasn't any time for that. By now the damned mechanism might already have been activated.

I spun around, throwing my left arm backward as I turned. My arm hit the Venezuelan's gun hand, and the gun fell from his hand and clattered on the floor. I jammed an elbow into his meaty face and connected solidly. There was a dull crack of bone, and he gave a loud grunt, then fell back against the wall and slid to the floor, where he sat dazed and moaning.

"Nick, for Christ's sake!" I heard the Secret Service man yell.

He lunged at me, and I turned to meet him, throwing a hard left into his face. It caught him, just right, and he went down.

The other Venezuelan had pulled his gun and was obviously planning to use it on me. He was aiming at my chest as I grabbed wildly for the gun hand. I shoved the gun up and to the right just as he pulled the trigger. The report reverberated, in the corridor, and slug crashed into the ceiling. I heard shouts coming from the far end of the hallway. In a minute every security man in the place would be on top of me.

I twisted hard at the Venezuelan's gun hand and finally managed to get the revolver away from him. I let it drop and jammed a knee into his groin. The man bent over double, screaming in pain. While he was still clutching at his crotch, I slammed the side of my hand against his head and connected, sending him flying against the conference room doors.

The first Venezuelan started to get up, but I kicked him in the side, and he fell heavily onto his back. I started to open the doors, but they were locked. I stepped back to kick them in.

"Hold it, Carter."

It was the Secret Service man. I turned to him only for a minute. He was aiming his .38 Smith &

Wesson at my chest. I looked at the gun, then back at him.

"I'm going to go into that room," I said evenly. "If I don't, everyone in there will die. You'll have to fire that damned thing to stop me."

I turned away from him, raised my foot, and kicked hard at the doors. With a loud crash they flew open, and I dashed into the conference room.

A door had hit a Secret Service man and knocked him to the floor. All the other security people started moving toward me, and the members of the conference looked up at me in alarm.

"What the hell is this?" the man on the floor shouted. He'd seen the guard on the floor out in the corridor.

The distinguished-looking Venezuelan President looked at me with restrained interest. The American Vice-President staring at me in open shock and fear.

"What's the meaning of all this?" It was an American aide who'd gotten up from the table. After their initial shock, everyone at the conference was becoming indignant.

"Please stay calm," I said in a firm voice. "That carafe on the table contains a deadly weapon. Its function is to kill everybody in this room."

Eleven

Everything was noise and confusion. Several men stood up hurriedly and scrambled away from their seats. I went in past them and leaned over the table.

"Get him" the Venezuelan from the corridor yelled.

I'd just about reached the carafe when a Venezuelan plainclothes man grabbed me from behind. I couldn't get to the carafe. I turned and fought wildly to free myself.

Just then the device was activated. Everybody in the room felt it—I could tell by their faces. There was no audible sound. The device was emitting sounds at a frequency where you couldn't tell if you were hearing or just feeling. But one thing was clear—it was working on every nerve fiber in our bodies. The sound penetrated to the very core of my brain, tearing and grating at my nerves, jarring them mercilessly, causing agonizing pain and nausea. The pain started in the head and chest, just like the terrible sensations I'd had for the past two days, but this was going to get a hell of a lot worse in a matter of seconds. A couple of men at the table were putting their hands uncertainly to their heads, and one had already fallen forward onto the table.

"Let me go, damn it!" I yelled at the Venezuelan.

He released his grip on me just long enough to throw a big fist into my face. It hit me hard, and I fell back onto the table. But by now the guard was feeling the effects of the death machine. He grabbed at his head. I slugged him hard in the face, and he went down.

I tried to ignore the mounting excruciating pain in my head and chest, fighting the nausea that was overcoming me. I climbed unsteadily up onto the table, grabbed the water carafe, and stumbled off the other side of the table with it.

I fell when I hit the floor and dropped the carafe. With extreme difficulty I crawled over to it and picked it up again, then staggered back to my feet.

At such close range the effects of the device were even more intense. I was reeling. I glanced at the Venezuelan President and saw he had slumped back in his chair, his eyes glazed. The American Vice-President was trying desperately to get out of his chair. Everyone else in the room was getting very sick very fast.

I stumbled over to a window and smashed the leaded panes with the carafe. I was just about to throw it through the broken glass when Hawk burst into the room.

"Stop whatever you're doing, or I'll blow a hole right through your head. I mean it."

I looked and he was aiming his Beretta at me. I saw the look on his face change when he felt the vibrations from the machine.

"This is an ultrasonic weapon," I said weakly. "I'm getting rid of it."

Without waiting to see whether he was going to pull the trigger, I turned my back on him and threw the carafe through the broken pane. It shattered more glass then fell to the pavement below, smashing to pieces.

Exhausted, I turned back to face Hawk. I was so weak I had to prop myself up against the windowsill. Suddenly I felt the pain subside, and my churning stomach began to calm down. I looked around the room and saw that others were feeling the relief, too. They were beginning to show signs of life. The Venezuelan President moved in his chair, and the American Vice-President put a hand to his forehead. I was sure they'd be all right. They hadn't been exposed long enough for really serious injury. But I suspected that we'd all have quite a hangover for the rest of the day.

The room was slowly regaining some semblance of normality. The conference members were recovering pretty well, looking around at each other with sick, confused expressions on their faces.

Hawk was walking toward me with his Beretta pointed at my chest. A couple of security men came up and flanked him. He stood right in front of me, still holding the gun on me. The men with him looked as if they'd shoot at the slightest provocation.

"First you knife one of your own colleagues, an old friend at that, and you threaten my life," Hawk shouted angrily. "Then you clobber the head of the Venezuelan Security Police. And now *this!*"

The man I'd knocked down on the way in came over to join the group, his face still twisted from the pain he'd undergone. "He claimed there was a weapon in the water carafe," the man said. "Then something terrible started happening in here. When he got rid of the carafe, whatever it was stopped."

"That's right," an American at the table said. "It stopped the minute he threw that carafe through the window."

"So what was in the carafe, Nick?" Hawk asked. "Or do you still maintain you're a revolutionary named Rafael Chávez?"

"How's Vincent, sir?" I asked, ignoring his question. "Did I . . . ?"

"Kill him?" Hawk finished for me. "No. He's going to be all right. You missed his liver by about half an inch."

"Thank God," I said dully. Now that the conference was saved, along with the lives of its principals, I felt total exhaustion come over me. I needed about a week of sleep. And I found I didn't much care what they thought of my explanations. "No sir, I realize now I'm not Chávez. I got my memory back prematurely, I think, when the jets flew over. They wanted me to remember, but not till I heard a lower-frequency signal from the device. Then I was supposed to know who I am and realize what I'd done."

"They?" Hawk said, studying my face.

"The people who detained me for two days," I said.

Hawk studied my eyes and apparently decided that I was acting like Nick Carter again. He holstered his gun and waved the other agents off. The Vice-President was walking over to us.

"What the hell happened in here?" he asked us.

The Venezuelan President got up out of his chair. He answered the Vice-President above the noise in the room. "It seems that this young man has just saved our lives. That is what has happened, señor Vice-President."

The Vice-President looked from the Venezuelan President back to me. "Yes," he said slowly. "I believe that pretty well sums it up. But what was that devilish thing you threw out the window, Nick?"

"I'm not sure, sir," I said. "But if we can go somewhere private for a minute, I'll be happy to give you my theories."

"A good idea," the Venezuelan President said. "Gentlemen, this conference will recess for one hour, and then we will reconvene here to conclude our business."

We had a very private meeting. The Venezuelan

President, the American Vice-President, Hawk, and I went to the security annex, and everyone else was asked to leave. The chief of the Venezuelan Security Police had already been taken to the headquarters for a treatment. In a few minutes I was alone with the two dignitaries and Hawk.

"You acted very quickly in there, young man," the Venezuelan President said, his hands clasped behind him as he spoke.

"Thank you, sir," I said.

"Nevertheless, Carter," the Vice-President spoke up, "you've got a lot of explaining to do. Someone told me it was you who brought the carafe into the room."

"I'm afraid that's right, sir," I answered.

Hawk grimaced. "It seems that Carter was kidnapped and persuaded to believe that he was a Venezuelan revolutionary intent on assassination," he said sourly. He lit up a long cigar and began pacing the room, hunched down in his tweed jacket.

"Very interesting," the Venezuelan President said. "And now your normal faculties have returned, Señor Carter?"

"Yes, sir."

The American Vice-President sat down on the edge of a desk. "That's all very nice for us here in this room. But when the press gets wind of this, they'll be screaming that an American agent sabotaged the conference and tried to assassinate the President and me."

"I agree," said Hawk. "This won't be easy to explain."

"That occurred to me, too, sir," I said to the Vice-President. "But we do have a couple of leads to the people who are really responsible."

"And who are they?" the President asked.

I remembered what Tanya had said that night in her apartment just before the drug knocked me out. I looked over at Hawk for clearance to tell them, and he nodded. "KGB," I said.

"*Qué demonio!*" muttered the President.

"Stall the press for twenty-four hours," I said. "I'll try to find them. After that we can see that the entire world press gets the story. The real story."

Hawk studied my face for a minute, then looked at the Vice-President. "Can we have that much time?"

The Vice-President raised his eyebrows. "With the help of the Venezuelan government," he said, turning to the President.

The President looked at me soberly. "I trust this young man. You will have my full cooperation. Please keep me advised. And now, señor Vice-President, I must see my staff before the conference resumes. I will see you in the conference room. Mr. Carter, if you can vindicate yourself, you will receive my country's highest honors."

Before I could protest, he was gone. The Vice-President got up from the desk and came over to me. "Now that it's all in the family, Nick, I feel I must voice one last thought."

"I think I know what it is," I said. "I have the

twenty-four hours on trust. Because I could really be a defector. Or maybe just a lunatic. After my time is up, I'm on my own."

"Something like that, Nick. You seem all right to me now. But security is security. There has to be some doubt in my mind. I hope you don't mind my speaking so frankly."

"I understand. I'd feel the same way, sir," I said.

"I'll stake my job on Carter," Hawk said suddenly, not looking at me. "I trust him implicitly."

"Of course," the Vice-President said. "But get moving on this one, David. The press won't wait forever."

The Vice-President left the room. Hawk and I were alone. After a long silence, I finally spoke.

"Look, I'm really sorry about all this," I said. "If I'd just been more careful with the girl . . ."

"Cut it out, Nick. You know that we can't guard against all eventualities. Anyway, I had you check her out. She was counting on that. Nobody could have avoided the trap you fell into. It was very well planned, and it was conceived by experts. Now, let's reconstruct what happened."

"Well, my best guess is that I was drugged and then . . . maybe hypnosis, I don't know. I really can't remember anything since that evening in the girl's apartment. The drug was in her . . . lipstick."

Hawk managed a small grin. "That's why you blame yourself. Don't be silly, my boy. But assuming this girl was a KGB agent and they took you to some secluded place to hypnotize you—why did they keep you for two days. Hypnosis would only take a few hours, at most. And how could they get you to do anything that went against your moral code? Hypnosis doesn't work that way."

"Well, I'm just guessing, but if they could have managed to change my whole personality, my entire identity, then my moral code would be altered along with it. If I really accepted the fact that I was a revolutionary who believed in the forcible overthrow of his government, the idea would work. And we know that the Russians are using behavior-control techniques that can completely break down a man's morals and integrity and make him a slave to conditioned response. A combination of hypnosis and behavior control could have convinced me I was Chávez."

"Yes," Hawk said thoughtfully. "And a damned clever idea it was. Take a top American agent, turn him into an automaton killer, and turn him loose to do some dirty work for you. Then let him and his country take the blame. I'm beginning to appreciate the threat in that warning note now."

"Which was written just to get us over here," I said.

"Exactly. And I fell for it—hook, line, and sinker. If anybody is to blame, Nick, it's me."

"I read the note, too," I said. "Maybe we'd better quit trying to place blame and start thinking about bringing this assignment to a close. We've destroyed their grand plan, but now we have to nail them." I looked at the floor. "I have an idea they're patting themselves on the back over this one and maybe getting a good laugh out of it. Well, the fun at my expense is over. When I find them, they won't be laughing."

"I suspect you've sobered them up some already," Hawk said, "since you aborted their multiple assassination attempt. How do you know the girl is KGB?"

"Because she told me," I said. "Or at least she admitted it when I asked her. That was just before the drug knocked me out. Anyway, her real name is Tanya Savitch, and she has a hint of Russian in her German accent. I couldn't quite identify it before the drug."

"Is that all you can remember about her?"

"At the moment. I have an apartment to check out and the German Embassy and a restaurant where I saw her. Also, I have a memory of a clinic and white-coated men and Tanya giving me instructions about all this. I can't remember their names or the things they did to me there. They blindfolded me when I left the clinic, so I have no idea where it is."

Hawk grimaced. "Well, at least you avoided the tragedy they had planned, Nick. You say you came out of your trance prematurely?"

"The jets going over made a sound similar to the one I was supposed to hear from the machine. That sound, along with the warning messages my subconscious had been sending for the past two days, made me to go to the window to hear the jets again. The KGB must have wanted me to return to my real identity after the assassination was over. If I denied I was Nick Carter, that might have confused the reporters. They wouldn't have known who was really responsible. Or they might have just figured I'd gone berserk. The KGB didn't want that. They were out to humiliate us, and they damn near succeeded."

"*Are* you all right now, Nick?" Hawk asked, watching me closely.

"I'm fine," I assured him. "But then, I'm supposed to be."

He grunted. "Okay. Is the girl our only lead?"

"The only good one. I remember something about that mystery man. Something new. I think he was at the clinic."

Hawk puffed at his smelly cigar and blew a smoke ring. "That figures. Well, you should probably have some tests first, but we don't have time for that now. Get on with it if you feel up to it."

"I'm up to it," I said. "But keep the police and the other agents away till my twenty-four hours are up. That's all I ask. I don't want to be stumbling over assistants."

"All right, Nick," Hawk said.

"Then I'll see you at your hotel."

I was seated across a large mahogany desk from Herr Ludwig Schmidt, the West German deputy ambassador, who was supposed to have taken Tanya to the reception the night I met her. Schmidt was reclining in his high-backed chair, a long cigarette in his right hand.

"Oh, yes. I took Fraulein Hoffmann to the reception. She wanted to attend a diplomatic function. She is a bright girl, you know. She called in sick right after the reception. Apparently she ate something at a bullfight that upset her stomach terribly. She has still not returned to work."

"How long has she been with you here?" I asked.

"Not long. A Hamburg girl, if I'm not mistaken. Her father was a Russian refugee."

"Is that what she told you?"

"Yes. She speaks German with a slight accent because of her family situation. Her family spoke Russian in the home."

"Yes," I said, "I see."

Herr Schmidt was a very thin, sexless man in his forties, obviously very satisfied with his role in life. "A lovely girl, don't you agree?" he asked.

I remembered the times I'd been with her on the sofa, cot, and bed. "A *very* lovely girl. Can I reach her at the address listed in your files?" It was the same place she'd taken me the night she'd drugged me.

"Why, I'm sure you can. She is ill, after all."

"Yes. In case I don't find her at home, do you know of anyplace else I might look? Restaurants or cafés or special places for relaxation?"

"But I have told you the girl is ill."

"Please," I said impatiently.

He seemed irritated by my insistence. "Well, I myself have taken her to lunch on occasion at a small café near here. I don't remember the name, but she likes the Venezuelan *hallaca,* and they serve it there. It is a cornmeal dish."

"I know," I said. I remembered that Tanya had ordered that at El Jardín after the bullfight.

Schmidt smugly stared at the ceiling. "Actually, I think the girl is attracted to me," he said confidentially. "Being a bachelor in this city is a delightfully consuming pastime."

"I suppose," I said. "Well, I'll try to find her at home, Herr Schmidt. Good afternoon to you."

He didn't get up. "My pleasure," he said. He stared up at the ceiling again, probably daydreaming about his sexual potential as an unmarried male in Caracas.

I really didn't expect to find Tanya at her apartment. She must have arranged to leave it the minute the last phase of the operation began—my capture. But I hoped I'd find some kind of clue there. I was met on the main floor of the building by a fat Venezuelan *portera* who didn't speak any English.

"*Buenas tardes, señor,*" she said loudly, a big grin on her face.

"*Buenas tardes,*" I answered. "I'm looking for a young woman named Ilse Hoffmann."

"Ah, yes. But she doesn't live here any more. She moved out very suddenly, several days ago. An unusual foreign girl, if you will excuse me for saying it."

I smiled. "Did she take everything with her?"

"I haven't checked the apartment carefully. There are so many apartments here, and I am a busy woman."

"Would you mind if I took a look upstairs?" I asked.

She gave me a hard look. "It is against the rules. Who are you, please?"

"Just a friend of Miss Hoffmann's," I said. I reached into my pocket and offered the woman a fistful of *bolívares*.

She looked at them, then back at me. She reached out and took the money, looking around her shoulder down the hall. "It is number eight," she said. "The door is unlocked."

"Thanks," I said.

I climbed the stairs to her apartment. With luck, I might be able to stop Tanya and her comrades before they caught a plane to Moscow. But I was worried—they undoubtedly knew by now that their plot had failed.

Upstairs, I entered the apartment. Memories crashed in on me again in rapid succession. The wide sofa sat in the middle of the room, just as it had on that night when Tanya had bartered her body for the capture of an American agent. I closed the door behind me and looked around. It was all so different now. It lacked the life, the vibrancy, that Tanya had given it. I rummaged through the drawers of a small desk and found nothing but a couple of theater tickets. They wouldn't do me much good in the next twenty-four hours. I moved on through the rest of the apartment. I went into the bedroom and found a crumpled bullfight program in the wastebasket there. I recognized Tanya's handwriting because she scribbled the notes on the program when I was with her at the bullfight. Just some kind of reminder to pick up groceries. It was worthless to me. I'd just thrown it back into the wastebasket when I heard a sound in the living room. The door to the corridor had opened and closed very quietly.

I reached for Wilhelmina and moved up tight against the wall beside the door. There was only silence from the other room. Somebody was stalking me. Somebody who had been watching the apartment building and was worried I'd get too close for comfort. Maybe it was Tanya herself. I heard an almost inaudible squeak of a board under the carpet. I knew the exact location of that board, since I'd stepped on it earlier myself. There didn't seem to be any reason to put off the confrontation. I stepped out into the doorway.

A man stood in the center of the room, holding a revolver. He was my mystery man, and the gun was the same one he'd pointed at my head in Washington and the one I now remembered seeing in the white corridor at the KGB laboratory. He whirled around when he heard me.

"Drop it," I said.

But he had other ideas. He fired. I realized he was going to shoot a split-second before the gun went off, and dived for the floor. The revolver barked out loudly in the room, and the slug slammed into the wall behind me as I hit the floor. The gun roared again and chipped up wood at my side as I rolled over and came up firing. I fired three times. The first slug smashed a lamp behind the gunman. The second entered his chest and drove him backward into the wall. The third shot caught him in the side of the face, just under the cheekbone, and blasted out the side of his head, spattering the wall with a crimson mess. He hit the floor hard, but he never even felt it. The man who had haunted me all through this mission was dead before his body knew it.

"Damn!" I muttered. I'd had a live witness, a man who could have told me everything. But I'd had to kill him.

I got to my feet quickly. People in the building would have heard the shots. I went over to the sprawled figure and looked through his pockets. Nothing. No I.D., false or otherwise. But there was a small scrawled message on a scrap of paper. It said merely:

T. La Masia. 1930.

I jammed the paper into my pocket and went to a window. I could hear footsteps and voices in the corridor. I pulled the window open and stepped out onto a fire escape. In minutes I was on the ground, leaving the building far behind me.

It was getting dark by the time I came out onto the street. The message on the note was turning over and over in my mind. There was a La Masia restaurant on Avenida Casanova. I stopped suddenly, remembering. I'd heard of the place because it was noted for its *hallaca,* Tanya's favorite Venezuelan dish, if she'd told me and her friend Ludwig the truth. Could it be, I wondered, that the *T* stood for Tanya and that the mystery man, apparently a Russian agent, intended to meet Tanya there at 19:30 hours—or 7:30 P.M.? It was the only lead I had, so I might as well follow it.

I arrived at the restaurant early. Tanya was nowhere in sight. I took a table at the rear, where I could see everything without being observed, and waited. At 7:32, Tanya walked in.

She was as beautiful as I'd remembered her. That much hadn't been an illusion. A waiter led her to a table near the front. Then she got up and walked down a small corridor toward the ladies' room. I got up and followed her.

She had already disappeared into the room marked *Damas* when I reached the small alcove. I waited there for her, glad that we'd be alone and away from the people in the dining room when she came out. In a minute the door opened, and we met face to face.

Before she could react, I grabbed her and shoved her hard against the wall. She gasped loudly.

"You!" she said. "What do you think you're doing? Let go of me or I'll scream."

I slapped her across the face with the back of my hand.

"What do you think this is, some kind of game in experimental psychology?" I growled at her. "You and I have a score to settle."

"If you say so, Nick," she said. She was holding her face with her hand. Her voice had softened.

"I say so, honey," I said. I let the stiletto drop into the palm of my right hand.

"You're going to . . . kill me?"

"Not unless you make it absolutely necessary," I said. "You and I are walking out of this place together. And you're going to act as if you're having a great time. Or you get this in the ribs. Believe me when I say I'll kill you if you try anything."

"Can you forget the times we were together?" she asked in that sensual voice.

"Don't con me, baby. What you did was all business. Now move. And act happy."

She sighed. "All right, Nick."

We got out of the restaurant without any trouble. She had come by car, so I made her take me to it. We got into it, and I sat behind the wheel. The car was parked on a dark side street, completely alone.

"Now. Who were you meeting at the restaurant?"

"I can't tell you that."

I shoved the knife up against her. "The hell you can't."

She looked terrified. "He's an agent."

"KGB?"

"Yes."

"And you are too?"

"Yes. But only because of my special knowledge —because I'm a scientist. I suited their purposes."

I started the car and drove out onto the Avenida

Casanova. "Which way to the clinic?" I asked. "And don't play games with me."

"If I take you there, they'll kill us both!" she said almost tearfully.

"Which way?" I repeated.

She was really upset. "Make a right turn ahead and follow the boulevard until I tell you where to turn again."

I made the turn.

"Where is Yuri?" she asked. "The one who was to meet me."

"He's dead," I said, not looking at her.

She turned and stared at me for a minute. When she looked ahead again, her eyes were glazed. "I told them you were too dangerous," she said almost inaudibly. "Now you've spoiled their grand plan."

"Well, maybe it wasn't all that grand," I said acidly. "Is Dimitrov the guy who directed this master scheme?"

She was shocked to learn that I knew Dimitrov's name. She was a real greenhorn in the business, in spite of her fancy credentials. "You know too much," she said.

"Will I find him at this so-called clinic?"

"I don't know," she said. "He may be gone by now. Turn left at the next street."

She gave me further directions and I followed them. As I made a hard right, she turned to me. "I want to know. What went wrong? When did you come out of hypnosis—and how?"

I glanced over at her and grinned. "I've been

going crazy guessing the truth for the past couple of days. Now I'll let *you* guess for a while."

At the next intersection we made a final turn to the left, and Tanya told me to stop in front of an old building. The ground level looked like an unused store, and the floors above seemed deserted.

"This is it," she said quietly.

I shut off the engine. Looking in the rear-view mirror, I saw another car pull up behind us. For a minute I thought it might be Tanya's friends, but then I recognized the square face behind the wheel. Hawk had borrowed a CIA man to have him keep an eye on me. My sudden anger subsided. I couldn't blame him, considering how I'd been behaving lately. I decided to ignore my watchdog.

"Get out," I said to Tanya, waving Wilhelmina at her.

We climbed out. Tanya was tense and really terrified.

"Nick, don't make me go in with you. I've shown you the headquarters. Please save me. Remember those moments we spent together. You can't forget that now."

"Oh, yes, I can," I said in a cold voice. I nudged her with the Luger, and she moved around the building to a side door.

None of it was familiar. I had been heavily drugged when they brought me and blindfolded when I came out. But I remembered the approximate distance from the street to the side door, and it was the same. Inside, when we climbed down a steep stairway to the basement level, I counted the same number of steps I'd counted when I'd left the clinic. There was no doubt about it—Tanya was leading me into the lion's den.

Twelve

As we entered the white corridor I began to re-member more and more isolated incidents. I had stood in this hallway before, and the man I had just killed in Tanya's apartment had held a gun on me here.

"You are remembering," Tanya said.

"Yes. There was a room, the orientation room. I was strapped to a chair."

"It is just ahead."

I moved on down the corridor. "There was an-other man," I said. "You and he worked together. I remember the name *Kalinin*."

"Yes," Tanya said heavily.

I opened the door Tanya had indicated, my Lug-er out and ready. I stepped inside with Tanya right in front of me. Memories came crashing in on me. The hypodermic. The hypnosis. The audio-visual sessions. Yes, they'd done a damn good job on me.

The chair with the straps and wires was still there in the center of the room. The machinery

was on the wall, but one piece was already partially dismantled. A technician stood beside it. I recognized him. The name *Menéndez* came to me. He
turned and stared at me uncomprehendingly for a
minute.

"*¡Mil rayos!*" he said, swearing darkly when he
realized his underground fortress had been penetrated.

"Hold it right there," I said, taking a couple of
steps toward him.

But he panicked. He started to grope in a drawer of a cabinet near him and came up with a gun.
It looked like a standard Beretta automatic. As he
turned toward me, I fired the Luger and hit him in
the heart. He went crashing back into the partly
dismantled machine, sprawling in a heap of arms
and legs, his eyes staring at the ceiling. A leg
twitched once, and he was dead.

A minute later I heard Tanya's voice behind me.
"And now it is your turn, Nick."

I turned and saw that she had gotten hold of a
revolver and was aiming it at me. I hadn't been
watching her closely because I simply hadn't figured her for the shooting kind. That was the second time I'd been wrong about her. There was an
unhappy but firm resolve in her face. As I raised
the Luger, her small gun exploded in the room and
the slug hit me. I spun in a tight circle, crashed
against the big chair, and fell to the floor. Fortu-
nately, her aim had been poor, and she'd hit my left
shoulder instead of my chest. I still had the Luger.

Tanya was aiming again, and I knew this time

her aim would be better. I couldn't play games with her. She had decided to make this a showdown. I fired the Luger and beat her to her second shot. Tanya clutched her stomach and, reeling backward, crumpled to the floor.

I got to my feet and went over to her. She was lying on her back, holding her hands over the bloody place on her abdomen. I swore under my breath. Her eyes were already showing the glaze of deep shock. She was trying unsuccessfully to breathe evenly.

"Why the hell did you have to do that?" I asked sadly.

"I . . . was too afraid, Nick. I could not go back to . . . Moscow a complete failure. I really . . . am sorry. I liked you so much." Her head rolled to one side, and she was dead

I knelt over her for a minute, remembering. Even in death, her face was beautiful. What a goddamn waste! I holstered the Luger, stood up, and went over to the cabinet where the technician had gotten his gun. I opened a couple of drawers and found records about my conditioning. Those, together with these machines, should just about tell the story. I'd make sure they sent press photographers here. The machinery alone would be headline material. I was as good as vindicated now. And it was the Kremlin, not Washington, that would be humiliated.

But where was Dimitrov? If he escaped now, this whole thing would leave a bad taste in my mouth. My job was a lot bigger than just embar-

rassing the Kremlin. I had to show the KGB
they'd gone too far on this one. It was a matter of
professional principle.

I heard footsteps in the corridor.

I slammed the cabinet drawer shut and drew
Wilhelmina once more. I heard the sound in the
corridor again. I went over to the door just as a
man ran past in the hall. It was Kalinin, Tanya's
colleague, running awkwardly with a heavy case
in one hand. He was almost at the end of the corridor.

"Stop!" I yelled.

But he kept running. The rats were fast desert-
ing the sinking ship. I fired the Luger and hit
him in the right leg. He went sprawling onto the
floor, just short of the exit leading to the stairway.

I heard a sound behind me. When I turned I saw
another man, the short, stocky one with the Khru-
shchev face—the other KGB Mokri Dela man. He
was aiming a revolver at me.

I flattened myself against the wall as he fired,
and the shot chipped into the wall just a few inch-
es from my head. Then I saw another man in the
corridor beyond the gunman, a taller man with
gray in his hair and a briefcase under his arm. It
was Oleg Dimitrov, the resident operator in
charge of the assassination mission. He was the
one I really wanted, the one I had to settle with before the KGB would really understand they
couldn't play games with AXE. He was running
very fast down the corridor toward the far end,
probably toward a second exit.

The Mokri Dela man fired again, and I crouched low just as the bullet whistled over my head. I shot back but missed. He aimed a third time, but I fired first and hit him in the groin. He screamed in pain and went down. But by then Dimitrov had disappeared at the other end of the hallway.

I ran to the fallen agent. He was writhing on the floor, sweat streaming down his face, ugly noises coming from his throat. He had forgotten all about the gun in his right hand. I kicked it out of his hand and ran down the corridor. He'd probably live to face trial. But I didn't think he'd be happy about it.

I followed Dimitrov into a room at the end of the corridor, but inside I saw an open window facing the alley. Dimitrov was gone.

I crawled painfully through the window into the dark alley just in time to see a black sedan roar out of the far end. I ran to the street and met the CIA man there.

"What the hell is going on, Carter?" he said.

I looked in the direction the black sedan had taken on the boulevard. I was sure it was headed for the airport. There was a flight to Rome within the hour. Dimitrov was probably planning to take it.

"There are some dead and injured Russians in there," I said. "Go see that the live ones stay put. I'm going to the airport to get their boss."

He looked at the blood running into my hand from my jacket sleeve. "My God, why didn't you take me in there with you?"

"Your job was just to watch me, not storm the fortress. Anyway, it would have taken too long to explain. See you at the debriefing."

I got into Tanya's car and drove away. If I was wrong and Dimitrov wasn't at the airport, I wouldn't have lost anything. I could put out a general alert for him and get the Venezuelan police in on the act. But I was pretty sure my hunch was right.

In twenty minutes I was at the airport. As I went into the terminal building, I remembered how large it was. It was built on several levels. Even if Dimitrov was there, I could very easily miss him. Unless I played my hunch on the Rome flight. It was a TWA flight, scheduled to leave in half an hour. I went to the ticket counter. Dimitrov was nowhere in sight, so I asked an agent about him, giving a full description.

"Why, yes. A man answering that description was here, except the man I saw had a mustache. He was here just a few minutes ago."

"Did he have any luggage?"

"He didn't check any, sir."

That figured. And the mustache would have been easy for Dimitrov.

"He gave the name of . . . Giorgio Carlotti, I think," the clerk said. "He had an Italian passport."

"And he just left?"

"Yes, sir."

I thanked him. Dimitrov was here, I was sure of it now. I could just go to the gate and wait for him to show, but that left quite a bit to luck. Besides, there would be a mob of travelers at the gate. It could get pretty messy there if Dimitrov decided to fight.

I looked around a nearby magazine shop, but Dimitrov wasn't there. Then I went to the currency-exchange window. I even went downstairs to the baggage checkroom and inquired. Dimitrov seemed to have disappeared.

I'd just turned a corner when I spotted him.

He was heading for the men's room, a briefcase under his arm. He hadn't seen me. The small gray mustache had changed his general appearance. It wasn't much of a disguise, but he hadn't had time for a better one.

Dimitrov went into the washroom, and the door swung shut behind him. This was it. I would have to hope that the washroom wasn't crowded.

I pulled out the Luger as I opened the door.

Inside, Dimitrov was just about to wash his hands at a sink across the small room. I looked around and was glad to see that there wasn't anyone else in the room. Dimitrov glanced in the mirror and saw my reflection in it. His face went gray with fear.

He spun to face me, reaching into his jacket as he turned. He was making a desperate try for his gun. I squeezed the trigger on the Luger and heard a dull click.

I glanced down at the gun. I knew the chamber was loaded. It had just misfired—a faulty cartridge, something that happened only once in a million times. I grabbed at the ejector with my bloody left hand.

But there was no time. Dimitrov had pulled a big Mauser Parabellum and was taking careful aim at my chest. He had dropped into a low crouch.

I dived for the tile floor. The slug hit tile beside my head and ricocheted around the room as I let Hugo slip down into my hand. I twisted sharply toward Dimitrov and let go with the stiletto. It sliced into his upper thigh.

I'd hoped for the torso, but I was probably lucky to have hit anything under the circumstances. Dimitrov yelled when the stiletto hit him, and his Mauser dropped to the floor. He pulled the long knife out of his leg and went for the lost gun.

In the meantime I'd ejected the bad cartridge from the Luger, and it clattered to the floor. I aimed at Dimitrov just as he was going for the Mauser. As he reached out toward it, he looked up and saw that he didn't stand a chance.

He put his hands up and backed away from the gun. Seeing the look on my face, he suddenly began talking. "All right, Mr. Carter. You win. I surrender to you."

I got to my feet, and he got up, too. We stood across the room from each other, our eyes locked in a hard stare. My left arm was beginning to ache terribly.

"You made a big mistake, Dimitrov," I said. "You picked AXE to humiliate."

"I demand to be turned over to the police," he

said. "I have surrendered to . . ." He lowered his hands slowly, then suddenly reached into his pocket, and a tiny Derringer appeared in his hand.

I squeezed the trigger on the Luger, and this time the gun fired. The slug caught Dimitrov just above the heart and hurled him back against the basin. His eyes stared wide at me for a moment, and then he grabbed spasmodically at the towel dispenser beside him. As he fell, the cloth towel came out of the dispenser in a long sheet, half-covering his inert body.

"Your Kremlin bosses can think about this one the next time they dream up a grand plan," I said to the corpse.

I stuffed the Luger back into its holster. I was just putting Hugo back in its sheath when two policemen charged through the door, their pistols drawn. They looked at Dimitrov and then at me with dark scowls.

"*¡Qué pasa aquí?*" shouted one.

I showed him my I.D. "Call the chief of the Security Police," I said. "Tell him the Russian conspirators have all been apprehended."

"Si, señor Carter," the man said.

I left the room and made my way through a mob of curious travelers to a nearby counter where I could place a call. I'd made a mental note of the location of the underground headquarters of the KGB, the bizarre laboratory where a fantastic experiment had been performed on a human guinea pig —me. Hawk would want to get over there to take over from the CIA man and to tell the police what had happened. He'd be sure the press got the story right.

I got a phone from the ticket agent but paused for a minute before dialing the number. I didn't like missions that ended with onstage performances. There would be more security meetings, and I'd have to give my story to a lot of people. I didn't need any of that just now. What I needed was an evening with a girl like Tanya Savitch. I was haunted by the sight of her lifeless body, still beautiful in death. KGB or not, she'd been very special.

I took a deep breath and let it out slowly. Well, maybe if I got lucky, there would be another brunette with deep blue eyes and a sensual, purring voice. And maybe she wouldn't be an enemy agent, and I wouldn't have to kill her. That was something to keep me going during the next few weeks of bureaucratic hassles.

I picked up the receiver and dialed Hawk's number.

AWARD

NICK CARTER

Don't Miss a Single
Killmaster Spy Chiller

CARNIVAL FOR KILLING　　　　Nick Carter
A fantastic espionage plot turns laughter to horror at
the Carnival in Rio.　　　　　　　　AS0938—75¢

ASSIGNMENT: ISRAEL　　　　　Nick Carter
A deranged Nazi threatens revenge and destruction in
the Middle East.　　　　　　　　　AS0939—75¢

THE CHINESE PAYMASTER　　　Nick Carter
Killmaster hunts a double agent who has set America
up for a takeover.　　　　　　　　AS0940—75¢.

THE DOOMSDAY FORMULA　　　Nick Carter
When the Japanese Communists threaten to sink
Hawaii to the bottom of the sea, the call goes out
for Nick Carter.　　　　　　　　　AS0941—75¢

THE CAIRO MAFIA　　　　　　Nick Carter
Tracking down secret plans for a deadly Russian
super-weapon, Nick fights the deadly New Brother-
hood in the shadow of the pyramids. AN1001—95¢

THE INCA DEATH SQUAD　　　Nick Carter
Trapped by Chicoms, pursued by Chilean guerrillas,
hounded by a fiendishly cruel and powerful Russian
minister—Nick must survive the ravages of a three-
sided death trap.　　　　　　　　AN1016—95¢

ASSAULT ON ENGLAND　　　　Nick Carter
With a beautiful British agent as his only ally, Nick
matches wits against a maniac master criminal intent
on systematically annihilating the entire English government.　　　　　　　　　　　AS1030—75¢

THE OMEGA TERROR　　　　　Nick Carter
An American defector plans to unleash a deadly
microscopic bug that would render the entire United
States lifeless, unless Killmaster can destroy him before "Omega Day".　　　　　　　AN1033—95¢

ICE BOMB ZERO　　　　　　　Nick Carter
Nick pits his strength against an elite corps of Chi-
coms, a treacherous spy, and the deadly Arctic cold!
　　　　　　　　　　　　　　　AN1088—95¢

More revealing and dramatic
than Inside The Third Reich!
"Utterly Fascinating...rich in
intriguing disclosures and
brimming over with
unconscious ironies"—The Atlantic

The Goebbels Diaries

Edited and translated by Louis P. Lochner

New In This Edition: Afterword by
Brigadier General Telford Taylor
Chief Counsel at the Nuremberg Trials

Written from the summit of power by Hitler's
maniacally brilliant Minister of Propaganda,
these diaries not only present a unique portrait
of the rulers of Nazi Germany, but reveal the
daily double-dealings, personal animosities, petty
jealousies, horrifying hatchet jobs and frighten-
ing national decisions that were all part of the
infamous world of the power elite inside the
Third Reich.

AY1161 $1.95

THE INCREDIBLE KRUPPS   Norbert Muhlen
The fascinating story of the gigantic munitions empire
that stormed through history. A stunning portrait of
the intimate scandals and bizarre perversions that were
essential parts of the Krupp family.

A550N   95¢

Action-Packed Westerns

THE GOOD, THE BAD, THE UGLY Joe Millard
They formed an alliance of hate to steal a fortune in dead man's gold! A blazing new Western! AX0918—60¢

A COFFIN FULL OF DOLLARS Joe Millard
The Man With No Name, Shadrach, Apachito—a legendary threesome out for each other's blood with a coffin full of dollars the winner's take-home pay! AX0856—60¢

FOR A FEW DOLLARS MORE Joe Millard
The trigger-tempered loner from the Award "Dollar" Western series matches wits and bullets with the most desperate gang in the West! AX0919—60¢

A DOLLAR TO DIE FOR Brian Fox
No men ever killed in colder blood than the desperate foursome led by the gun-ready hero, The Man With No Name! AX0917—60¢

DEAD RINGER Brian Fox
Two fast-talking, sharp-shooting mavericks—more brash and wild than Butch Cassidy and The Sundance Kid! Based on the ABC-TV series "Alias Smith & Jones." AS0896—75¢

LAWMAN Grant Freeling
He lived his own brand of justice—and his star was a license to kill! Now a major motion picture starring Burt Lancaster, Robert Ryan, Lee J. Cobb. AS0851—75¢

THE GUNFIGHTER Martin Ryerson
Morgan Royal, a two-fisted lawman—the man who had hunted down Quantrill after the Civil War—challenges a gang of killers ... and is trapped in a powdersmoke hell! AX0653—60¢

SECRET MISSION: NORTH KOREA
Don Smith

Sherman is ordered to command a crew of thieves, perverts and murderers on a lethal mission of reprisal. They must blow up a North Korean harbor—if Sherman can keep his men from killing each other!

AX0616—60¢

SECRET MISSION: ANGOLA
Don Smith

With a price on his head for a murder he didn't commit, agent Phil Sherman tries to save a man he never met, for the future of a country that isn't his . . .

ANII53 .95¢

SECRET MISSION: MUNICH
Don Smith

Millions in counterfeit dollars are bankrolling a dangerous neo-Nazi gang. Sherman must find and destroy the money factory—and the new Nazi leaders!

AS0727—75¢

SECRET MISSION: ATHENS
Don Smith

Bone-chilling danger and deadly treachery—the name of the game that Phil Sherman is playing for keeps in Assignment No. 11.

AS0801—75¢

SECRET MISSION: THE KREMLIN PLOT
Don Smith

A dead Russian skyjacker . . . a vital Soviet secret . . . and Phil Sherman becomes a moving target as four big powers move in for the kill!

AS0866—75¢